To Eileen
love Liz.

CW00798763

Throne of Shame

Best wishes

Fran Norton

Dedication

This book is in memory of my mother.

This above all: to thine own self be true.
Hamlet
Act I Scene 3

Throne of Shame

FRAN NORTON

Ellingham Press

British Library Cataloguing in Publication Data

A catalogue record for this book is available from the British Library

ISBN 978-0-9570781-3-0

Typeset by ISB Typesetting, Sheffield, UK

Printed by Lightning Source UK

Ellingham Press, 43 High Street, Much Wenlock, Shropshire TF13 6AD

www.ellinghampress.co.uk

CONTENTS

EXPLANATORY NOTES

Ordinances	Based on terms drawn up in the Magna Carta in the reign of King John to address the grievances of the earls and magnates of the kingdom.
Ordainers	Made up of eight earls, seven bishops and six barons.
Perambulation of the forests	Land which over generations had been encroached upon by the monarchy for royal hunting. It involved many hundreds, if not thousands, of acres of land throughout the kingdom. The land, not legally owned by the Crown, had reduced the income of landowners for many years, giving rise to great resentment.
Squires	Young boys from noble families sent into households to learn the art of knighthood. They were assigned to various categories either to serve the earl or noble as a personal attendant or at table or to see his armour was in good order or to attend the expensive horses owned by his lord.
Pantler	Servant in charge of the bread and the pantry.
Charger	The schooled warhorse of a knight.
Destrier	The agile horse used in tournaments.
Sumpter	Horse of burden.
Caltrap (or caltrop)	Weapon in the shape of a cross mounted on three steps, used to lame horses and infantry.
Murrain	Virulent disease in cattle not unlike foot and mouth.

In some instances place names are spelt as in medieval times.

ACKNOWLEDGEMENTS

First I wish to express my gratitude to the late Stuart Timmins for his detailed booklet on the LeStrange family, to Dr Paul Martin Remfry for translating a passage in medieval Latin regarding Alice, to Hugh Wood for his help on heraldry, to members of the Mortimer History Society, to Shrewsbury Archives, to Liz Phillips for her assistance with suggestions and editing, and to my husband Tony for his help.

I would also like to say a special thank you to Ellingham Press, Ina, Heidi and Colin, and to Gareth B Thomas who so kindly allowed me to use the image on the back cover from a stained glass window in St Laurence's Church in Ludlow.

I would also like to express my thanks for the support of members of the Shrewsbury Society of St George, especially its President Sir Charles Soame Bt. Last, but certainly by no means least a big thank you to Clive and Barbara Blakeway, who have proved the words of the old adage – friends in need are friends in deed – and I was certainly the friend in need!

PREFACE

Throughout medieval Europe the success or failure of a nation rested solely on the character of its king, but even a powerful monarch needed the support of his nobles, his family and the Church.

Edward I, aptly described in Marc Morris's book *A Great and Terrible King*, was indeed a successful medieval king. His ruthless reputation began at the Battle of Evesham where he did not just defeat his uncle Simon de Montfort, but where his order of 'no quarter' was a clear message to any would-be adversaries that, unlike his father Henry III, the future king of England was a fearsome opponent.

Upon his succession Edward surrounded himself with men of vision and ability, foremost amongst whose numbers was Henry de Lacy. The king was also fortunate in his Plantagenet family and held the loyalty of his uncle Richard, Earl of Cornwall, and his brother Edmund, Earl of Lancaster, Leicester and Derby. Their indispensable support enabled Edward to show a united front in the field of conflict as well as around the council tables of Europe.

The king also used marriage to bind lands, titles and wealth to his family, thus underpinning their powerful position. Henry de Lacy, Earl of Lincoln, with only a surviving daughter to inherit his vast wealth and titles, was delighted when a marriage was arranged between his daughter Alice and the king's nephew, Thomas Plantagenet. Henry saw this move as a way of securing his daughter's future – he little realised the true nature of his prospective son-in-law.

Old age blunted none of Edward's ambitions, which were no longer confined to Europe and Wales, but also included Scotland. Here, however, his dominance was challenged and the Scottish issue proved far more difficult than he first anticipated.

Edward I was also faced by the most heart-wrenching fact that his son and heir Edward, Prince of Wales, possessed none of the traits necessary to be a successful king. He also had misgivings about his nephew Thomas.

Throne of Shame is set within the framework of actual historical events and follows the life of Alice de Lacy as she travels through a time which sees England during its most controversial period. Human frailties blight a nation, bringing about strife and civil wars. How Alice and her lady-in-waiting Matty face the vagaries of the age is revealed in these pages.

I therefore extend an invitation to accompany Alice through one of history's most turbulent, eventful periods, littered with colourful, controversial characters.

BOOK ONE

THE KING'S GREAT CAUSE

CHAPTER I

Pontefract Castle
1292

A pair of pale-grey eyes watched the colourful cavalcade draw ever closer to the great castle of Pontefract. The slender girl shuddered and clenched her tiny hands. Edmund Plantagenet, the Earl of Lancaster, also styled Comte de Champagne and known as 'Crouchback', was quite easily identified astride his richly caparisoned steed. Beside him rode his fourteen-year-old son and heir Thomas. Bright pennons, gonfalons and banners fluttered all around the royal party, and even from this distance Alice could hear voices and the jingle of harness. 'Heralds are unnecessary, methinks!' she exclaimed softly so only her attendant heard.

Matilda knew the dread in which this forthcoming betrothal was held by her young mistress. 'He is a powerful magnate and will...'

The girl raised her tiny hand to silence the sentence. 'My lord Plantagenet is gaining much more than a mere wife. My father is forfeiting lands, wealth and titles for this match. My only hope is that you are allowed to accompany me in my new life.' She spoke hesitantly.

Matilda Holden, affectionately known as Matty, had been Alice de Lacy's nursemaid since her own widowhood and she too much feared a separation. Grief was hard enough to bear, but for this girl who had recently lost both brothers most cruelly she felt a knot of anxiety. Would this wrench from her home be a wound too many? She had witnessed the change in the once merry girl. The bright smile which had frequently lit up the pale face had disappeared. Nowadays Alice wore a solemn, silent air of loneliness. The young woman understood all too well the pain of loss: her own husband had been slain in a skirmish at Dryslwyn Castle five years since, and the grief grew no less hard to bear with the passing of time.

'They will be here anon! I must don my fine apparel or incur the vexation of my mother.' The pair exchanged an understanding look as the girl held out her hand to be helped from her vantage point.

'We shall wear finery that all mismatches and watch the effect.'

Matty smiled. Slight and small she might be but Alice de Lacy had spirit and fire. True, the sadness had dimmed its flame for some months, but Matty knew it still burned beneath the surface and could but wonder at how this child would grow and deal with a life she did not wish for in a marriage she did not want! With no time to dwell on idle thoughts, she must make Alice ready for this important ceremony. The mighty Earl of Lancaster was here to formalise the betrothal to Alice, the sole heiress of Henry de Lacy, Earl of Lincoln and Denbigh, and his wife, Margaret Longespee, Countess of Salisbury.

The earldom of Lincoln had been bestowed on Henry by Edward I in 1278 for his faithful and loyal service, together with the honour of Pontefract. Henry was a valued advisor and doughty soldier and as such held the esteem of Edward and his court. The loss of his sons John and Edmund left Alice as the only surviving child of this powerful nobleman and his austere wife. A marriage to the son of the royal house of Plantagenet would, he felt sure, secure the future of their daughter.

Alice entered the Great Hall holding her head high; she looked neither to her left or right. She knew her appearance would cause her mother to gasp. The yellow surcoat and grey kirtle did nothing to complement the pale skin; in fact it made her look sallow and sickly. But Edmund Plantagenet, Earl of Lancaster, rose and stepped forward extending his hand in greeting.

'Lady Alice, this is a great occasion and we welcome you as our beloved daughter.'

Alice took the proffered hand and as he raised it to his lips she noted his piercing eyes and deep baritone voice. He was dressed exquisitely in the French fashion, for he spent much time in France. Edmund's wife was the handsome Blanche of Artois, daughter of the powerful Count Robert Artois. Alice felt ill at ease but tried desperately not to reveal her true feelings to this great prince, unaware that her tiny hand trembled in his. He smiled down at her. 'Do not fear us. We are well pleased with this match and look forward to you becoming a member of our family.'

Henry de Lacy moved to his daughter's side. 'In the circumstances we had hoped you would allow Alice to remain here with us until the formal wedding. The loss of my sons has afforded us much sorrow…'

He did not continue as Edmund nodded. 'Of course, of course! It is natural for a family to grieve together.'

As he spoke, Alice looked under her lashes at the figure that was to be her future husband. Thomas Plantagenet possessed an air of haughty arrogance, a trait which would work against him in his adult life. The girl saw in the youth nothing which pleased her eye. He was tall with the stamp of Plantagenet upon his features, but the mouth was weak and he rarely looked anyone in the eye. Alice thought it a shifty trait. However, she did not miss the covert gaze as he scanned the hall, his attention lingering on the women, especially the pretty ones. He deliberately ignored her presence and flicked his sleeve as his father spoke as though the event was of no import to him, and she knew he did it for her benefit. She was of little consequence to this royal youth. Alice felt her anger rise but she was at pains not to show it! *So, Master Arrogance, you think to treat a de Lacy with no respect. We shall see! We shall see!*

The rest of the ceremony continued, and as the minstrels struck up Margaret Longespee hissed in Alice's ear. 'What manner of dress is this? What has become of the blue-and-gold surcoat and the kirtle of red? That serving woman of yours will be well punished.'

Alice was truly in awe of her mother and answered quietly, 'Pray do not punish Matty, I spilled a goblet of wine over the ones she had laid out and had to wear these or not appear at all!' She crossed her fingers at the untruth and hoped she betrayed nothing of it to her mother.

'We will talk of this later, now go and speak to your future bridegroom.' With that she turned on her heel to rejoin her husband and honoured guests. Alice neither heard the melodic tones of the minstrels nor indeed remembered the sumptuous banquet served, as all she could think about was her future with Master Arrogance. Even as she pondered her thoughts she saw him manoeuvre one of the serving wenches into a darkened corner and fondle her breasts. Hateful, ignorant youth!

The following day was spent hunting on the surrounding moors where the company enjoyed great sport. Edmund 'Crouchback' proudly watched his son despatch a mighty boar. 'Well done, sirrah! He surely led us a merry dance!' The elegant Earl of Lancaster turned to Alice who sat passively watching the scene before her. She noted the intensity and venom in the flushed features of the young Plantagenet. Thomas had great delight in the kill and did not flinch when one of the horses and two of the hounds were badly gored in the chase as the wounded boar turned and charged them. Unfeeling brute! Alice felt uneasy at these emotions which came unbidden, for they would not prove conducive to an amicable marriage. Try as she might she could not staunch the notion which she knew would fester like a wound untreated.

'Come, let us leave the huntsmen to their work and return to rest before this evening's festivities.' Henry de Lacy raised his hand to the rest of the company and swung his great bay horse on a homeward course.

'Ah, my dear earl, we have all enjoyed a good day's sport. However, I am not so sure about your daughter!' Edmund smiled sympathetically towards the straight-backed girl who rode her spirited mare with innate ease.

'Alice is no faint-hearted female believe me, my lord! But she has a soft place in her heart for most animals.'

Why did Alice flinch inwardly at her father's statement? She saw Thomas Plantagenet's eyes narrow at the words. Now she would not be able to own a pet dog or horse or in fact show any special feelings towards anything, for in so doing she might give this selfish, arrogant youth a weapon against her! As she rode homewards Alice felt a deep feeling of impending doom. She would be friendless and alone tied by bonds of the Church and the law in a union which even now she feared. Maybe he would die! Like her two brothers, Edmund and John. Fall down a well and break his neck or fall from a parapet. *Why did* they *have to die and leave her?* It was a question Alice kept asking herself but without any satisfactory answers. Coupled with the growing feelings towards her future bridegroom, Alice enjoyed nothing of the remaining days of festivities. In fact, Alice felt she had more in common with one of the dancing bears, whose chains clanked at each step and whose pitiable expression reflected her own pangs of resentment.

A week later, Alice watched the resplendent party ride out through the gates of Pontefract and breathed a great sigh of relief. Now for at least a while longer she could return to the normal pattern of her life. However, her mother gave instructions for extra lessons of etiquette and deportment and ordered a new wardrobe of expensive garments. Dancing was also a feature of this new routine and Alice often ached with her efforts. Undaunted, her desire to succeed and to surpass all her mother's expectations never wavered for she would not give 'Master Arrogance' cause to tease or scorn a de Lacy. Matty admired her young mistress's efforts and watched the transformation unfold as Alice grew from a child into a graceful girl.

'I swear you have grown inches these past months!' Matty exclaimed as she stitched at the hem of a dark-green kirtle.

Alice smiled. 'I hope I grow tall enough to look at "Master Arrogance" directly in the eye for I would not have him look down on me.'

'Oh, mistress, I have prayed that you would bury your dislike of your husband to be…'

'Then I fear your prayers have gone unanswered.' Alice flashed one of her rare smiles at Matty and continued, 'Now were it his brother Henry, who was far more courteous and personable… I would have been quite reconciled to a marriage with that Plantagenet.'

Matty knew her attempts to alter her young mistress's feelings towards the heir to the Earl of Lancaster were futile. Nevertheless she would persevere, for a life in constant conflict, whether on a battlefield or in a marriage, boded ill for the combatants. She loved Alice dearly and was aware of the enmity a strained relationship could cause.

Alice's education continued apace and she applied herself unstintingly to the onerous daily tasks. Her dead brothers could not fly the de Lacy standard into battle, but the young heiress had vowed to uphold the honour of the de Lacys in their memory. Her only respite during that period was when she was hunting, for she revelled in riding across the wild countryside and watching her young merlin swoop onto its prey. She would return from the field bright-eyed, glowing and energised, and Matty rejoiced on such occasions. The other pursuit Alice found enjoyment in was music, especially in the melodic notes of the harp and lute. Maybe it harkened back to the years of childhood when many Welsh mercenaries possessed the skills not only of war, but also of music, for their haunting ballads had frequently echoed around the castle walls at Denbigh.

Alice grew from a gauche child into an assured young girl ever conscious that she too had Plantagenet blood flowing through her veins and was as royal as her bridegroom, albeit from the wrong side of the blanket. Alice was also descended from the Italian nobility; her great-grandfather was Manfred III, Marquess of Saluzzo, whilst on her mother's side was the great William Longespee, 'Longsword', the illegitimate son of Henry II. She must never forget her lineage; such knowledge could be a defence, even a weapon, for had she not learned from her father: words used wisely could prove more lethal than a sword...

Nonetheless, Alice felt fearful of her impending marriage. It was a fear she could neither explain, nor understand – a deep-rooted premonition which would not be quenched even though she prayed fervently for strength to overcome its powerful hold. But through these troubling times there was also a new experience, one of choosing the semblance of her own household: huntsmen, grooms and harpers, for Alice's delight in music grew daily and her light tuneful voice would often be heard when she thought she was unobserved. Already a good horsewoman, she rode with confidence and grace. Even though she was light in years it was well noted that Alice could outride many on the hunting field. She was in fact quite an unusual young noblewoman, more at ease in the company of her groom or falconer and the household servants than she was with visiting magnates. Her informal air was a trait inherited from her father, although Henry was at ease in the presence of all men, whatever their station of birth.

However, such informality did not apply to the Countess of Salisbury. Alice's mother held the world at arm's length and secretly abhorred her husband's familiar manner. Nonetheless, Margaret Longespee had come to appreciate his unique qualities and knew that this unconfrontational approach had often diffused many a difficult situation in council, for the king's abrasive personality frequently angered his earls, barons and prelates – how fortunate he was to have men such as her husband to smooth his way. But what the countess condoned in her husband's case, she was not about to allow her daughter to do. She sent for Alice to inform her thus!

Whilst Alice was being admonished by her imperious mother, Henry de Lacy sat at his large oak desk tapping his quill against the inkwell. Scattered across the desk were many scrolls and letters, some opened, some with seals as yet unbroken. Since the death of England's chancellor, Robert Burnell, Bishop of Bath and Wells, and close friend to the king, many of his duties now fell to Henry.

The autumn of 1292 had proved a grievous season for the king who had lost his valued chancellor at Berwick during the negotiations with the Scots. This blow had come a mere two years after the loss of his beloved wife Eleanor. Burnell had understood the needs of Edward's subjects in the great debates of the day and upheld the view that the voice of the 'Commons' should be equally as loud as that of the nobility. He stated quite simply, '*That which the law touches should have a say in such laws.*' The king had accepted the wisdom of his chancellor, for the two men thought alike on so many issues.

'I fear we shall be held fast to our task for many hours, Luke, for I believe these raids in the Channel are merely a forerunner of a more serious conflict.'

'Aye, my lord!' Luke Lytton looked up from his work; ink stained his long fingers and fine sand dusted his faded tunic. Henry cleared his throat and placed his quill in its slot. He rose and stood before his young scribe. 'There is a matter that lies close to my heart which has little to do with the king's affairs but nonetheless is one I judge of import to me.' Luke looked expectantly at his master. Henry began to pace the flagged floor and resumed, slowly glancing from time to time towards the seated figure. 'As you are aware my daughter will be married in the fullness of time and I have learned that she is somewhat circumspect of this union. At this moment she is considering those that she would take into her new life and as the future Countess of Lancaster such positions will be much sort after.' As Henry gazed out of the window he went on slowly, 'I would like you to accompany her, Luke.' He turned to watch the effect his words had on the young man. Luke's expression did not alter and showed none of his inner emotion. Henry continued, 'I have great faith in your loyalty and discretion and this is not a position I would entrust lightly. As we both know, the court is rife with conflict and envy and as the future premier earl of England Thomas Plantagenet will be a target for many with ambitions and grievances and therefore may place the Lady Alice in a vulnerable position. Naturally, as her father, I wish to know that she has in her household those who will serve her faithfully, and on whom I can rely to advise me as to her welfare. The position of personal secretary to my daughter is not, I suppose, one as prestigious as to an earl. However, it is one I would take as a personal favour.' He passed Luke's desk, then went on again, 'I do not want your reply directly; take time to consider. We will speak of this again, but for now let us press on with the matters of state.'

As Luke continued with his work, his mind raced round the earl's request. The position as Lady Alice's secretary was in itself an honour and as the earl had stated it would be in a household at the heart of England's nobility and the hub of court life. It was a big decision as his own ambitions had been to rise in the service of the Earl of Lincoln and not that of his daughter. However, as one from such humble beginnings Luke recognised the significance of this personal request by his esteemed master and allowed himself a feeling of pride.

CHAPTER II

Lincoln Castle
28 October 1294

Late autumn tinged the countryside with rich hues of reds and russets, the once-bright green grasses and rich, dark heathers now turned to muted browns. The skies, whose fickle clouds frequently ran before blustering winds and dashing rains, also heralded the mood of change in the young heiress.

The day of the wedding dawned, a day Alice had dreaded for so long. She had prepared meticulously for the great occasion. As she gazed at her reflection she had a sense of disbelief.

'Come Matty, tell me true, how do I look? Don't cozen me for you know I abhor lies.'

'You look like a great lady, all grown and elegant. The Lincoln-green velvet becomes you and your hair has never shone brighter.' Matty's eyes filled with tears.

'My hair may shine, but my heart does not!' Alice's voice was low and heavy.

'Then we must trust in the Lord, my lady, our lives are his to command.'

Alice turned and looked hard at her maid. 'I often wonder if he looks down on mortals like pieces on a gaming board and moves us around to see how we will react.'

Matty crossed herself hastily. 'Why, mistress, you should not be thinking such thoughts. He has a purpose for us all and we must pray for the strength to fulfil that purpose.'

Alice moved to where Matty stood and planted an affectionate kiss on her cheek. 'What would I do without you, Matty?' she said smiling wistfully. 'At least I shall not be expected to become a wife in the "expected" sense this night as I have yet to see my first flux.

So that at least will serve as a comfort. However, my breasts are swelling so no doubt all the other female traits will quickly follow!' Alice sat quite still to let Matty weave and fix jewels in her hair.

Matty tried to comfort her mistress. 'You know young Thomas is not ill-looking in fact…'

'Matty! Please do not speak of "Master Arrogance" in glowing terms. I swear I shall vomit!' Alice's tone was sharp and unfamiliar. 'I have watched him parade around the castle, have seen him in the lists and at his sword practice and know that if he makes a blunder he strikes his servant or tutor. This is not the behaviour of a true knight. In fact, he appears to be quite free with his fists and feet, a trait I find most unseemly. In truth I have only ever witnessed my father strike a man but once, and that for abusing an animal. No, Matty, Master Arrogance will have to work hard at redeeming himself if he is ever to find favour in my eyes!'

Matty continued with her task, her deft fingers plaiting strands of the thick wavy hair until the effect was quite enchanting. Pearls and emeralds encircled the crown whilst topaz and pearls fanned out down the locks complementing the Lincoln-green kirtle and gold surcoat. At her throat Alice wore the heavy gold locket embossed with the de Lacy knot given to her by her paternal grandmother, Aleisia of Saluzzo. The Italian workmanship was quite superb in its intricacy.

Finally the hour had come and Alice and Matty walked the long corridors to the increasing volume of the choir. Alice caught Matty's hand for an instant. 'Pray for me!'

Matty could not speak, just nodded, for she always kept Alice in her prayers as she truly loved her mistress above all others.

'Well, let us show how a de Lacy can perform ceremonial duties.'

Alice, flanked by pages in the livery of the de Lacy family walked without haste to where the great gathering of magnates, earls, barons and prelates had assembled to witness the formalisation of the wedding of Thomas Plantagenet, nephew to the king, to the daughter of one of England's most respected noblemen, Henry de Lacy, Earl of Lincoln.

The fanfare heralding the king rang out round the high roof and the clamour of voices was silenced as the procession began to wend its way towards the great altar. The notes died away to be replaced by the melodic chanting of the monks and choir. Alice clenched her hands and the closed expression she had learned to adopt in public spread over her pale face. Her glorious hair rippled down her back and framed the fragile features. Her large, pale-grey eyes held an unfathomable gaze as she focused on the high altar where the figure of Thomas Plantagenet now stood resplendent in a dark-blue velvet tunic edged in ermine, the sign of royalty. Alice stood beside her father as he took her hand to place it in the clammy grasp of her bridegroom. Alice repeated the oath of marriage but within her heart she felt a defiance which almost threatened to overwhelm her. As Thomas spoke the final vows she reclaimed her self-control and when she turned to walk down the aisle as a wife, no one in the assembly but Matty Holden had an inkling of Alice's true state of mind.

The king was well pleased with this marriage, for it brought to his brother's son the de Lacy wealth and titles of Lincoln and Salisbury to add to those of Lancaster and Leicester. This was a strategy Edward I adopted whenever and wherever possible and one his late wife, Queen Eleanor, also used for the benefit of her kinsmen and -women. Wealth and lands were all-important and the closer he was able to bind his most influential nobles to the crown the better it had suited the royal couple. Monies expended on wars throughout his reign left England's coffers empty, and the populace suffered through heavy taxation. There was a constant need to supply grain, horses, wagons and men to replenish whatever was required to service the armies. The latest war in Gascony was yet another drain on the exchequer, but Edward saw it as a necessary move in his grand scheme of things. Money would be found – *must be found*.

Today, however, was given over to celebrations and Edward was determined to enjoy this break from war and drank many toasts to the health and future of the young couple. Throughout the feasting Alice remained impassive and only when the king led her onto the floor in a stately dance did Alice's talents as a dancer shine for all to witness. She moved elegantly and lightly through the steps, the candle glow burnishing her dark-brown hair with rivers of flames, her eyes glowing in the reflected light tinting her pale features into honeyed hues. Matty gasped; Alice looked unreal, like a spirit from another world gliding through the musical notes in rhythm to the beat.

'So, Lady Alice, your dancing skills are truly delightful.' Edward smiled down at the girl.

'I thank you, sire!' Alice inclined her head slightly at the compliment.

'And will you fill the royal nursery with many offspring?' he quipped.

'To answer that question, sire, you will have to speak with God, for I do not possess an answer. Besides, I have not yet reached the necessary stage of womanhood needed to achieve pregnancy, I believe.'

Edward laughed out loud at her reply. 'And under that slight frame I do detect a wit worthy of a de Lacy.'

'I sincerely hope so, sire!'

As the dance ended Edward led the young bride to the dais where Thomas and his family sat watching. Alice noted the smiles of Thomas's parents and the encouraging expression on young Henry Plantagenet's face which was not, however, reflected in the features of his older brother.

'Come now, Thomas, it is your turn to lead your new wife in a dance.' The king gave Alice's hand to Thomas.

'I leave the prancing to others,' he said sulkily, his voice already thick from drink, and quaffed another goblet of wine in one draught.

A frown flickered across Edward's brow as he noted the look of concern on Henry de Lacy's face. The look was sufficient to silence the rebuttal which had been upon his lips. Instead he smiled stiffly as he continued, 'Then your father shall take your place.' Edward turned to Edmund whose face was etched by tiredness.

'Sire, I pray to be excused.' He looked up at Alice. 'Forgive me, daughter, I could not match such talent. Besides I have found today's events somewhat tiring.'

Alice smiled understandingly at him. 'Dancing should be enjoyed, my lord, not endured.'

It was young Henry Plantagenet who rose and held out his hand. 'Then may I have the honour of dancing with my new sister?'

Alice smiled, totally unaware of how lovely she looked. Together the two young people took to the floor and danced the night away, lost in the magic of the music. Alice was completely at ease, even though she was being watched with interest by all the guests.

When the couple finally returned to their places, Thomas was nowhere to be seen. He was busy deflowering one of the unfortunate young wenches who had been serving wine.

'Have you been deserted already, Lady Alice?' The words were spoken by a dark-haired young Gascon who sat beside the Prince of Wales. Alice looked enquiringly at the speaker.

'Ah, pray allow me introduce myself. My name is Piers Gaveston.'

Alice noted the handsome features and eyes as black as jet. She also noted the lazy smile which curved round the lips of the young Prince of Wales.

'Come, Piers, you must not tease the young bride. Methinks Thomas has but gone to…relieve himself!' The two smiled at each other in a knowing fashion. Henry Plantagenet came and stood beside Alice. She felt grateful for his support; so why then did she feel so disconcerted?

'Ha! You see, Lady Alice, you have a valiant champion to come to your rescue!'

'I did not know I needed rescuing, Master Gaveston.' Alice stood quite still, not showing her nervousness.

'Pray leave Mistress Alice. Remember, Piers, she is a de Lacy and to incur my father's displeasure at upsetting the earl's daughter on such a night could bode ill for both of us!' The Prince of Wales caught Pier's elbow.

'Do you feel I have insulted you, Lady Alice?'

'No!' Alice said softly. 'However, I think you may have maligned my husband's reputation, therefore I feel sure that on his learning of this he may… seek some explanation.' Alice saw the Gascon's smile widen.

'Then pray dance with me to show there are no ill feelings, for I truly admire courage, and from a dainty maid whose looks belie such spirit, I do doubly bow in honour.'

Alice hesitated, but when she spoke, only those close could heard her words.

'A de Lacy is not so easily gulled, sir! I therefore decline your offer and know you understand the refusal!'

The smile did not slip from the handsome countenance as he leaned forward and whispered softly, 'Beware, lady, for you have entered the Plantagenet web and we who are caught in its mesh must tread carefully.' Without a backward glance he had moved to catch up with his royal companion.

Margaret Longespee had noted all the unfolding events and had stared as though awakening from a long trance. What had they done? This royal marriage which she and her husband had long congratulated themselves on now appeared to her in a different light. She had been so locked into her own grief at the loss of her children – Edmund, John, and more recently young Margaret – that Alice's fate had quite simply been blotted from her conscience.

Now she awakened to the fact that Alice had been married to a spoiled, vindictive, unprincipled youth and she was completely powerless to do aught about it. Silently she voiced a prayer. 'May God have mercy my beloved daughter and may she forgive my lack of care.' She rose and left the Great Hall, nodding towards her hosts.

'What ails your wife, Lincoln?' The king looked concerned as he spoke. The death of his beloved Eleanor just two years before had made him far more aware of the vagaries of sudden illness.

'Pray do not concern yourself, highness; she did not sleep well last night!' Henry de Lacy was not lying, for although Margaret had not complained of her disturbed night Henry, through years of soldiering, now slept lightly and any untoward noise awakened him.

'Ah, just so, just so!' murmured the king and continued his deep conversation with his brother. Many of the male guests knew that they were bound for Gascony within weeks of this royal ceremony. Young Thomas Plantagenet would also be among their number, joining both his father and his father-in-law, Henry de Lacy.

As soon as he was able to escape from the celebrations Henry went to the chamber he was sharing with his wife.

'The king noted you leaving. Is aught amiss, lady?' Henry muttered gruffly. The sight of his wife's hunched figure made him uneasy. Margaret was usually so unemotional and in control. Now she looked frail and vulnerable.

'Oh, Henry, what have we done, you and I?' Tears rolled slowly down her pale cheeks.

'Madam! Come, come, this is not like you! What are we supposed to have done?'

'I saw it all tonight! Our daughter has been sacrificed on the altar of ambition.'

'What? What nonsense is this? Our daughter has married into the royal dynasty of Plantagenet.'

'That is true, but to a Plantagenet that has inherited all the weaknesses and faults of that breed.' She stared long and hard at her husband. 'Alice is an innocent, bright spirit, and he will ruin her.' At this Margaret Longespee began to sob uncontrollably.

The earl stood unable to answer for what seemed like an age, then he spoke slowly. 'You think I had a choice, lady?' His voice had lowered almost to a whisper. 'Believe me, since I first learned of this marriage proposal I have tried to think of the positive side of such a match. One day Alice will become the premier countess of England and as such will be cared for…' His words were stemmed by an outcry from his wife, a sound he had never heard before. It was like some primeval creature and the sound made his blood run cold. 'Margaret…please! I pray you, do not weep so!' It was rare that Henry de Lacy did not know what action to take or what words to use but he was lost for both at the sight of his normally reserved wife acting so out of character.

'I have made arrangements for certain trusted members of our household to go with Alice into her new life and report to me if aught goes amiss with her! I can do no more.'

Margaret wiped her eyes and raised her head. 'And when you are away, my lord?' Margaret's tear-stained face stared at him as she spoke.

'Then she must know that you and my mother are there for her support.'

The earl sat beside his wife and placed his arm about her shoulders. 'Our daughter may be but a slip of a girl but she has all the courage and wit of a Longespee and a de Lacy and may even come to influence her husband into becoming a better man.'

Margaret leaned against her husbands shoulder in a rare moment of intimacy. 'Then to those ends I will pray for her strength and protection.' She patted his knee. 'Not often is my shield of self-control lowered, my lord.'

Tentatively the doughty knight kissed his wife's brow, then rose. 'I must return to the celebrations. Do you wish me to make your excuses?'

'Just give me a little time and I will return.'

As the earl walked slowly back to the Great Hall he felt troubled.

He and his wife no longer shared a marriage bed and he failed to shake off the niggling feeling of guilt, for Henry de Lacy had taken a mistress some years ago and had until this moment felt no shame in the arrangement. Now a worm of doubt crept into his mind. However, by the time he reached the noisy festivities he was once again in control of his erring emotions.

'Ah, Lincoln, is all well?'

'Aye, highness, a slight faintness that is all. The countess will return directly.'

'Good, good, then let the merriment continue unabated.'

When Margaret Longespee returned, no one noted aught amiss, but Henry de Lacy was much disturbed by this unexpected turn of events.

Alice, on the other hand, was being chaperoned by her new brother-in-law, young Henry Plantagenet, who was busy pointing out various dignitaries that were amongst the guests. Some Alice already knew, but there many young squires she had never met.

'Slower, I shall never retain all these names, but some of their fathers will have served with my father, therefore I will know a little of their family histories.'

'If truth be told, we have so many squires attached to our household I can scarce keep apace with them all.' He smiled as he spoke, a friendly, open smile, which endeared him even more to the young bride. Alice liked her brother-in-law and was acutely aware of the enormous gap in the character and behaviour of the two sons of the Earl of Lancaster. The younger boy enjoyed his role as Alice's guide, introducing her with pride and dignity.

The scene was not lost on the dark gaze of Piers Gaveston. Although his companion, the Prince of Wales, always appeared on easy terms with his cousin Thomas, Piers did not hold the same feelings towards the royal youth. In fact, he felt the exact opposite. He neither liked nor trusted this Plantagenet, an instinct which would prove all too accurate.

The week of festivities quickly passed, ending with the exodus to all parts of the realm of the guests, many whose future was once again to don the apparel of war. This time, the destination was Gascony, although many Marcher barons were left to keep the ever restless Welsh in check. As the retinue of Edmund, Earl of Lancaster, and his son Thomas rode through the mighty gateway, Alice let out a sigh of relief and turned to Matty.

'Mama has invited me to accompany her to Canford. Can you believe it, Matty? Invited me! No command or insistence.'

'You are a wife now, therefore your station has changed. She is merely following the new order of events.' Matty was busy packing all the finery away as she spoke.

'I know, Matty, but I feel strange at the change in attitude. I am glad I wasn't expected to accompany Thomas.' She could not call him husband for in her heart she had not truly given him her oath. She would speak with Father Benedict on the matter for Alice held fast to her Catholic faith, and her conscience was uneasy at her lack of loyalty to this new marriage.

On the journey to Dorset Alice travelled in a litter with her mother. Matty, on the other hand, found herself with the other ladies-in-waiting in a far less luxurious litter, and the journey was anything but comfortable. As the journey progressed Alice became aware of the abject poverty of the peasants they passed. The emaciated faces and thin spidery arms of the children touched the girl in a way she had never felt before.

'These people...' she hesitated, searching for her words. 'How have they come to this state?' She looked at her mother, the concern she felt etched on her fine features.

'The vagaries and ambitions of a king dictate events, which in turn affect the lives of all his subjects, high- and low-born. The latter always bear the harshness of those effects, I fear. War is an expensive pursuit, but one the king feels is necessary for his realm. The sacrifice of his people on the altar of his ambition is the sad but inevitable outcome. Your father tries to point out this cost to the people – for the exchequer is quite, quite empty – but the king is oblivious and chooses to ignore facts he does wish to acknowledge. Therefore, it leaves his chancellor and councillors with the unenviable task of raising yet more taxes from a nation that is virtually bankrupt.' Margaret Longespee had never spoken to her daughter on matters of state before and Alice felt that at last her mother had acknowledged that she was of an age to understand her future responsibilities.

They continued on their journey in virtual silence, but both were mindful that they would eat good, wholesome food that night and sleep in warm, comfortable beds, unlike many of the peasants they had passed on their journey south, many of whom would not even see the morning.

Days after their arrival at Canford, Margaret Longespee sent for her daughter. Alice had returned from her daily ride and as she entered the comfortable but richly decorated chamber, noted the presence of her own secretary, Luke Lytton, as well as her mother's ageing cleric, Brother Ignatius.

'Come, Alice, there is a matter I wish you to know of and one which has been close to my heart for some time – that of inheritance!'

Alice stood stock-still, a look of alarm on her flushed cheeks. 'Is aught amiss?'

'No, no, child, do not concern yourself, my health is well enough. It is just now that we are here and without any interference from either your father or husband I will dictate in your presence how I wish to leave the lands and estates that are mine by right and not attached to the title of Salisbury which has been added to that of Lincoln in your marriage contract and will be legally under your husband's control. I wish to leave, to my beloved daughter, jewels and lands that belong to me and not included in any contract your father has made. The income relating to these will be yours solely to administer for your own benefit. There will of course be a few legacies which I know you, with the aid of Brother Ignatius...' she paused and indicated to the seated cleric whose quill was already busily scratching across a long parchment scroll. Seated on the opposite side of the large table sat the tall, slim figure of Luke Lytton, who was also similarly engaged on copying out the countess's instructions. For some minutes the austere figure dictated her will as she paced up and down the large, high-vaulted chamber. Alice had moved to the padded window seat and watched her mother with awe. When she had ceased talking she walked round and signed both scrolls with a flourishing stroke of the quill.

'Now we can relax.' She looked across at Alice and spoke in a softer tone. 'I feel that I have enabled you to be as financially independent as the law allows. This inheritance shall be yours and yours alone, Alice. No matter what pressures are brought to bear on you to give precedence to your husband, I shall make it legally impossible for him to lay any claim to these lands and titles and the income appertaining to them. Sadly, the majority of the Salisbury estates will go to your husband on my death as part of the marriage contract, but enough will be left for you to be financially independent.' She waved her hand to the scribes and they left clutching their documents, seals, quills and sanders.

Margaret turned to Alice. 'I can only protect you on matters of finance. However, my real concerns are in your personal life. My marriage to your father was political, but has been one of respect, something I now fear you may not have in your marriage.' She walked towards the crackling fire and spread her fingers towards its glowing warmth. 'This coming generation of Plantagenets has marked flaws and ones which time will not cure. True, the king is ruthlessly ambitious and warlike, but he nonetheless holds the respect of his nobles and prelates. Argue they may on many counts, but they know that they thwart him at their peril. His son...' she hesitated, then continued, 'will never possess such qualities. I can foresee sometime in the future a struggle for power, for I remember all too well the de Montfort wars, and suffice it to say your husband Thomas will be one of the protagonists.' She began her restless pacing as she spoke. 'He lacks the intelligence, the foresight and the loyalty his father commands and struts around the court more like the king's heir than the Prince of Wales has ever done. Between these two young men lies your future, Alice, and it will not be an easy one, of that I am certain. However, I have no control over their shortcomings and know that in my daughter lies the Longespee and de Lacy courage; in that and God I must trust.'

Alice ran across the chamber to clasp her mother's icy hand and kissed it.

'Come, emotions are best held close, Alice. Remember, an unguarded look or gesture can betray your inner feelings and enemies will circle like wolves and miss nothing of any show of weakness.'

'But I do not need to guard them from you, surely?'

The countess looked into the pleading face of her daughter and in a rare moment kissed her cheek. 'Now let us have some refreshment and we will speak no more of such serious matters.'

Alice would often remember this day throughout her life for her mother's good counsel.

CHAPTER III

The Savoy Palace
1296

The sunlight slanted across the stone floor encircling the figure who stood engrossed in a letter held in shaking hands. Kneeling before her was a liveried messenger whose tunic still bore the mire and dust of his long journey.

''Tis sad tidings you carry!'

'Yes, my lady.'

'Does the king know?'

There was a little smile of pride across his dusty face. 'Mine is the faster horse and I believe you have the news before the king, my Lady Alice.'

'And what is the name of my speedy messenger?'

'Kit...' He stammered, then corrected himself. 'Christopher Cavendish, my lady.'

'Then, Kit Cavendish, you and your steed shall be well rewarded. Now go to the kitchens for refreshments. Tomorrow come to me after Matins when I shall have more messages for you and your good steed to carry for me!'

The proud young man rose and bowed as he retreated, leaving Alice de Lacy pondering on the content of the letter. Her father-in-law Edmund Plantagenet, Earl of Lancaster and Leicester, was dead. This news now meant that her husband Thomas succeeded to the title after the due process of succession to his titles had been sanctioned by the king. That in turn made her the new countess. Alice called for Matty, who had been busily stitching at the far end of the salon. 'Matty, I have learned that my father-in-law is dead.' She hesitated. 'The wheel of life is turning on its new course.'

Matty crossed herself before she spoke 'And your...husband?'

'Will no doubt be more unbearable than before.' The two exchanged a knowing look.

'Did the earl die in battle?' Matty folded the silks into the fine linen bag and carefully put her needles into their case.

'Of a persistent fever – remember my father wrote of a delay in boarding the ship to France because of the earl's malady. It appears that he never really recovered and the bouts became more severe until they finally consumed him. Poor man, may God rest his soul.' Alice walked to the casement and looked out across the neat lawns. 'His body is being brought back as soon as arrangements can be made. I can imagine the grief of the Lady Blanche.' The two knew their lives would never be the same again. Alice would step into the role of premier countess of England and Matty would be elevated to senior lady-in-waiting. Both would now be elevated to positions with which neither would feel at ease.

'I think a prayer for our future and for the soul of the king's dead brother is in order,' whispered Alice. There was another fear that gripped her; now she could no longer claim her childhood as a block to the marriage bed for in the past months she had become a woman by all the laws of nature and she would no longer be free of her conjugal duties, a thought that filled her full of dread. Nevertheless, there were more pressing matters, for she would need to have fine mourning garments for the state funeral for the late Earl of Lancaster and to prepare for all her new duties.

On her next meeting with her husband, all of Alice's latent fears were realised and visible for the world to see. Thomas paraded around, haughtily ordering all and sundry to his bidding. He gazed at Alice with a new interest and his words left her in no doubt of his intentions.

'Ah, madam, I can see that you have bloomed since last we met and I shall send for you ere long to grace the marriage bed.' Alice indicated she had heard but remained silent. 'Your duty is to provide an heir and to serve me as a dutiful wife.' No preamble, no expression of personal sorrow at the loss of his father. Thomas Plantagenet was now Thomas, Earl of Lancaster and Leicester, and premier earl of the realm, and he was already making sure that all should know of his elevation in title and authority.

When Alice met with her grieving mother-in-law, Blanche of Artois, she noted a new face amongst her ladies-in-waiting: pretty, voluptuous and pert with round, blue eyes which boldly roved over the young countess and her lady-in-waiting.

Alice extended her hands in greeting. 'It is a sad return I fear, madam!'

The hands of her mother-in-law were icy. Blanche of Artois' normally lovely face was pale and drawn and her usual incessant chattering silenced. She merely nodded and tears welled in her eyes and ran silently down her face. 'My beloved Edmund!' was all she said.

Alice broke the silence. 'I see you have a new addition to your retinue.'

Blanche looked towards Alice's gaze. 'Ah, yes! May I present Yolanda Artois, my cousin.' She hesitated over the last few words of introduction. Yolanda Artois stepped forward and made an exaggerated curtsey to Alice.

'Countess, it is my pleasure to meet with you!' There was no mistaking the sensuality of this young woman. It sizzled around her like a lightning storm.

'Is this your first visit to England?'

'Yes – indeed I find your English fashions quite quaint.' She smiled and rolled her eyes as she spoke.

'Then you are used to the French court, no doubt?' Alice said softly. Before Yolanda could reply, Thomas strode into the room unannounced and his eyes alighted on the young French woman who returned his gaze for an instant, then dropped a curtsey.

'My lord, it is a great pleasure to meet with my cousin at last.' Her accent was heavy, but attractively so!

Thomas raised an eyebrow and turned to his mother for an explanation. But Blanche was not forthcoming and merely turned her cheek for her son's greeting.

'Is Henry here?'

'No, but is expected any day.'

'Then pray forgive me, I am tired and wish to retire,' and without further ado Blanche swept from the chamber, leaving Alice and Thomas alone with their attendants, along with Yolanda.

Thomas bowed. 'Lady!' he said offhandedly to his wife, his eyes, however, focused on his new-found kinswoman to whom he was far more effusive, kissing her hand and gazing into her eyes. Alice noted the exchange as she left their company and walked slowly to her chamber.

When the other servants had been dismissed Alice looked at Matty enquiringly. 'Well, what did you make of the new arrival?' She removed her headdress as she spoke.

'Trouble! She will set the young squires' heads awhirl, that's for sure!'

Alice nodded, then said softly, 'And Thomas among their numbers, methinks!'

A few nights later, Alice was visited by her husband. Their first encounter with the marriage bed was to have a profound affect on her life, for Thomas had arrived full of wine and aggression. He enjoyed taunting her and she felt like one of the animals in a fighting ring. After he tired of his drunken groping he brutally raped her. When she tried to protest at his behaviour she had received a series of stunning blows for her pains. As he humiliated her, he merely laughed sardonically at her tears. 'Now you know thy lord and master, madam, and remember I hold your very existence in my grasp!' He hissed the words, venomous in their intensity, and with that he lurched from her bedchamber.

Matty Holden found her mistress in a blood-soaked bed with fearsome injuries to her face, breasts and thighs. 'God have mercy!' she cried, then called for the young page Noah to send for a physician. Her instructions were clear: not one from the household. Noah found an aged surgeon, and through the night, after Ralph the old physician had given Alice a draught of the poppy to make her sleep, he and Matty bathed and dressed the multitude of injuries whilst she was unconscious, and applied all their skills of healing to the broken girl.

'You have knowledge of the curative powers of plants?' The old man watched Matty as she used lavender oil mixed in the waters to wash the bloody bruises and gashes.

'A skill learned from my mother.' She spoke without looking up at his craggy face.

'I too learned of such cures but from many leagues away in the Holy Land.' He shook his head slowly. 'The injuries we can see will heal; however, it is the ones which lie deep within the womb which I fear may never be healed.'

The two looked at each other with a mutual understanding.

'Your mistress will never carry a child to full term and if she falls pregnant...' he paused before continuing, 'could well lose her life. I have stemmed the bleeding, but...' He washed his hands as he spoke.

Matty wept silently as she took in his words. 'What manner of man would do such a cruel thing to his own wife and to the dearest maid?'

'The power of drink unleashes the lustful demons which lie within. I have witnessed the cruelty of men on the Crusades, all in the name of God, and often wondered, would God have wished such brutality in his name? I think not.' His spoke more to himself than to Matty. 'Who can say what his intentions were. He probably could not answer. She will sleep now for many hours, which will help. I will return on the morrow and we can see how she fares then. You have the healing ways and your mistress can be grateful for such skills. Now, godnight, child.'

Matty nodded and quietly let him out of the chamber. Pulling her truckle bed closer to her sleeping mistress she lay listening in the quiet darkness to heavy breathing. Matty prayed and turned over a germ of an idea which both troubled and comforted her through that long night's vigil.

The following day rumours flew around the Savoy Palace about the events of the previous night. Thomas, totally unaware of the mayhem he had brought about, was busy renewing his acquaintance with Yolanda Artois. The mutual attraction was immediate: for Thomas, the voluptuous body promised physical delights, and the young Frenchwoman found the tall, dark-eyed Plantagenet to her taste. It worried her not one jot that he was married or that they were so closely related by blood. She had been the result of lust and the fire of sensuality burned hot within her body. She realised it must have been the same for her mother who now lived in a comfortable chateau and enjoyed all the comforts any noblewoman would have due to the ties of blood with the Count d'Artois. Yolanda had every intention of finding a wealthy nobleman either to marry or to become his valued mistress. Already well versed in the art of pleasure, Yolanda was set on a course to make her own life a far more comfortable one than being a mere lady-in-waiting to her half-cousin. She had been sent from France after a scandalous affair with a member of her mother's household. The count had persuaded his legitimate daughter Blanche into taking the wayward offspring to England. Yolanda had merely been enjoying a sexual adventure and had delighted in the powerful young body of her mother's groom. Love had no place in her life – ambition burned too bright and she knew she had the body to excite men and was about to use those skills in bringing the very willing young Thomas of Lancaster to her will.

Over the coming weeks before the funeral of Edmund Plantagenet, the late Earl of Lancaster and Leicester, the lives of the two young women took very different paths. Alice de Lacy, her visual wounds healed, took her place in society. Her pale face concealed all the inner turmoil she felt and only her confessor, Brother Benedict, knew how shamed and stained she felt. The little cleric had tried to assure her the sin and shame were not hers and that God's love was ever bountiful and forgiving. He could not really say whether his words had been of help to his patron, but her strength of character to show nothing of her inner struggle prompted extra prayers on his young mistress's behalf.

Meantime, Yolanda Artois had indeed become Thomas of Lancaster's mistress and she revelled in this lustful and passionate relationship wholeheartedly. Already she had received expensive gifts and intended to furnish herself with many more. Thomas for once was both affable and almost jocular at times. He had at last found a young woman with sexual appetites to match his own. Many of the serving women of the noble households were safe, at least for the present, from the attentions of the young earl.

On the occasion of the sumptuous funeral Alice stood beside her husband, but they only spoke to each other when etiquette dictated. The young countess appeared remote and self-contained. Gracefully she walked in the procession behind the great, ornate coffin, looking neither to her right nor left. Her black funeral garments clung to her slender frame and her surcote, decorated with the de Lacy knot motif stitched in gold, glittered and shone at every step.

The king and his sister-in-law Blanche walked immediately behind the heavily draped coffin. Edward deeply mourned the death of his brother Edmund, who had throughout his life been much more than a brother to him. Friend, councillor, ambassador and soldier, always ready to serve him and the realm.

Edward mused during the long service; they were all beginning to leave him: his beloved wife Eleanor, his trusted friend and chancellor Robert Burnell and now his own brother. He was acutely aware of their unswerving loyalty and love which he knew would never be replaced. Lincoln, Gloucester, Hereford, and Warwick remained, but no one could fill the great chasm left by those that had gone to serve God. All he could do was show his utmost respect and gratitude, in a manner understood by all generations to demonstrate the honour in which he had held his dead brother.

During the feast that night Edward surveyed the younger generation who sat chattering, their laughter much more subdued than normal, as they enjoyed the delicacies before them. Edward studied his son the Prince of Wales and his ever-present companion Piers Gaveston. Next to them sat his nephew Thomas, successor to the titles of Lancaster and Leicester, with his young wife Alice, who sat passive and silent amidst the noisy guests. She only seemed to respond with any sort of animation when young Henry Plantagenet, the younger of his brother's two children, spoke to her. Now that was a young sprig of the family tree that promised much more than did the boastful Thomas; pity he was the second-born son. Edward felt the weight of his years that night, unhappy at the prospect of leaving his throne to a son who, even at this young age, was showing no appetite for the future role as king. A weak-willed son and a nephew whose own high opinion of himself outran any real qualities, in fact there was nothing to commend either of the young royal males to the ageing monarch, although he could not deny his affection towards them.

Soon after the mourners and guests made ready to leave London, Alice sought an audience with her husband. She found him sprawled on a heavy couch playing dice with a number of his squires and sitting watching them was the Lady Yolanda.

Alice stood for a second knowing her husband was aware of her presence but had chosen to ignore her. The indignation she felt threatened to overwhelm her, but the iron grip on her emotions held fast.

'Sir, I have received word that my mother is indisposed and has requested me to attend her.'

Thomas dragged his eyes away from the game board and looked at the girl standing before him. 'Am I about to add the title of Salisbury to my list?'

His callous words cut Alice deeply but her face showed nothing. 'I do not know whether she is sick unto death but feel it is my duty to attend her as my father is out of the country on the king's business.'

Her words had brought the fact of her father's important position to Thomas's attention. Suddenly aware that he was under scrutiny he struggled to regain the upper hand and appear in control and magnanimous. With a sickly smile smearing his lips he nodded and said so all could hear, 'Of course, my dear, you should go immediately and set your mind at ease. I shall instruct some of my squires to accompany you!'

Alice, relieved that he had not thwarted her request, curtseyed and left her husband who turned to the remaining company and said sarcastically, 'One must always seek to please the ladies – what?' The laughter was nothing if not strained, but Thomas noticed nothing amiss and carried on with his diversion.

His wife, on the other hand, moved with all haste to leave for Bolingbroke. As promised, two of Thomas's squires were in attendance, Fulke Somery and Hugh de Freyne. The former was a son of one of the Plantagenet household and the latter a young squire recently arrived from Artois. Alice elected to ride and made it perfectly obvious that she was not wholly pleased at being accompanied by her husband's squires, as she felt they had been sent to spy on her movements. Nevertheless, the freedom of the journey helped to raise her spirits and Matty was also more than happy, even though somewhat uncomfortable in the litter to which she had been relegated!

On their first evening's stop Matty noted that Alice had eaten all of the tasty venison pie and had even nibbled at a sweetmeat. As she helped Alice bathe and make ready for the night she felt emboldened to speak more freely than she had of late. 'My lady has regained some of her former spirits, for which I am heartily pleased!'

Alice looked at her attendant as she spoke. 'I'm afraid I have been lost to my own emotions.' She continued falteringly at first.

'Brother Benedict tried to placate me with his ministrations but as we both know,' she turned and looked straight at Matty, 'the Church blames all women for the fall from Eden. I felt even more shamed and damned after speaking with him after...after...'

Matty leaned across the large bath tub and held her mistress's hand. 'Lady, I am but an ignorant maidservant but I do know that it was not your sin. I have watched hatred burn into your heart and understand its reason but...' She hesitated, not knowing if she was being too forward. 'Hatred and revenge have a nasty habit of rebounding. Do not let it destroy the sweet lady I have loved from her childhood. Disdain and contempt can serve equally effectively and these can be put aside at will.'

Alice looked hard at her lady-in-waiting. 'Matty!' she exclaimed, 'such wise words. I know I have been locked in a dungeon of fear and anguish but I also know that I will not allow Thomas Plantagenet to ruin my life. He may have ruined my body but my spirit...never!'

Matty bent to clasp her mistress in her arms. 'Oh, my dearest lady, it is so good to hear you say such words. I have watched your hurt and pain and prayed for your deliverance from evil.' The two young women hugged each other, lost in their human affection, ignoring protocol and station.

As they continued on the journey the weather closed in and a bleak wind tugged mercilessly at their cloaks and threatened to whip off their headwear, but for Alice the weather matched her mood; she was now free from the constraints of the past weeks where she had been under the gaze of those at court. She rode with confidence and even laughed at some of her retinue's struggle with their garments. For Fulke Somery the journey was just another uncomfortable duty. However, for the swarthy Hugh de Freyne the countess's oblivion to the elements and her prowess as horsewoman ignited a new-found admiration within him. This young English noblewoman was a revelation to Hugh; she had been indisposed for a number of weeks and he had only recently arrived from Gascony as part of the escort for Edmund of Lancaster's body. He had quickly realised the gaping difference between Earl Edmund and his eldest son Thomas. Life for Hugh had changed so swiftly since his arrival in England. The young Plantagenet earl was lusty, arrogant and a hard-drinking youth somewhat akin to Hugh's own appetites. He immediately felt in tune with his new life and had been delighted by this commission to escort the countess.

For his part knighthood was surely the path to wealth and acclaim, and Hugh was bent on a course prepared to pay whatever cost it would take to attain his goal. Being in such a large household would be difficult, for he had been made acutely aware of his inferior position on his arrival. He had been jeered at until he had shown his fearsome fighting skills, and many had received bloody wounds and noses, which had quickly silenced any further taunts. Thomas had become aware of this new foreign squire from his mother's homeland and had shown his approval when he had selected him to escort his wife, making it quite plain he wanted to know her every move and encounter on her visit. Hugh knew his fortunes lay with the young earl whose ambitions would mark out Hugh's own future. Service in the household of a royal earl had already proved profitable, for he had gained a purse full of silver for this mission and hoped it was only the first of many he would earn in the service of Thomas of Lancaster.

CHAPTER IV

Cheswardine Castle
1296

'Will these wretched wars ever end?' Maud LeStrange looked at her husband as she spoke. 'Heaven defend us! Now I learn that Scotland will be the next in the offing!'

'My dearest wife, I should not worry yourself over Scotland, Wales is ever our priority and I wish for just a little respite from conflict here at Cheswardine. It is the only place on the Welsh Marches that knows the meaning of peaceful times.'

Maud sat punching her needle in and out of her tapestry. 'I fear for young Eubolo. In the household of the Earl of Lancaster he will surely be called on to serve even though he is but a decade old.'

'An honour to have been chosen...' His words were cut short by Maud's loud sigh of disapproval.

'Honour or not, my cousin has sent word that this young earl has none of the courtly attributes of his father.' She hesitated, then continued, 'In fact...he is a womaniser, and she hints that his treatment of the young de Lacy wife of his was nothing short of scandalous.'

John LeStrange looked hard at his wife. 'Have a care, lady, the Plantagenets have long memories and cruel tempers.'

Maud's dark eyes flashed. 'Then are you saying that all the long years of unswerveable loyalty of your family would stand for naught?'

'Aye, I am saying just that! Remember, lady, it is your son that will suffer should any loose-tongued gossip get back to the earl and, believe me, Eubolo's life would be worth not a fig.'

The words hit Maud hard and she stitched furiously in her

frustration. But Maud was not a woman to be thwarted by a man, especially her husband, and she was determined to question her son on their next meeting. However, she had taken her husband's words of warning to heart and vowed not to jeopardise her son's future with her careless gossip.

Life at Cheswardine was a boon and Maud appreciated the few weeks of tranquillity. Her husband had so recently escaped with his life after a fierce battle near their castle at Knockyn. Now she was free to enjoy days of hunting and of tending her garden, albeit she governed what the gardeners would plant and sow. Maud loved this place above all others; nowhere else could she move unhindered by fear of kidnap, death or reprisals, only here at Cheswardine. Knockyn lay in ruins. Ellesmere was favoured more by her husband's brothers and their families. Norfolk, the original seat of the LeStrange family, was now rarely visited thanks to her husband's constant duties here on the Marches, but Maud was a pragmatic woman and had learned to take each new day for its own worth and enjoy its treasures, for there had been many times of war and fear – enough for any woman's lifetime. She shrugged off her wandering thoughts. How many other women throughout the kingdom had just such similar thoughts? She was among the lucky ones. Her sons were hail and healthy, her husband respected, brave and in his own gruff way – kind! He treated his tenants fairly so she was much luckier than most. As she stooped to pick the bright gilly flowers she offered up a little prayer for the young Countess of Lancaster who by all accounts was not in so fortunate a position as was she.

Just as Maud LeStrange was busily picking her perfumed flowers her son Eubolo was watching the sword master wield a mighty two-handed blade. The air hummed with a whoosh as the silver weapon pierced the gloom. The boy sucked in his breath as he watched Master 'Strongarm' demonstrate his dexterity. He made a fearsome sight, for he stood two yards high and given the old warrior's reputation on the field of battle was hailed a hero especially by the squires in the household of the Earl of Lancaster. The old crusader had fought in every war until age and a serious leg wound in ⌒ curtailed his career in the service of the king. Howe skills as a swordsman were being put to good use, fo teaching the eager young squires who stood agape at his skill and mastery of the sword they saw before them.

'A well-balanced blade is essential. If you do not have this you will be dead within a heartbeat!' He stood for a moment, the mighty blade still, as he watched his audience. 'The sword should be an extension of your arm…but…with death as its greeting.' He grinned, a great, broad, yellow-toothed grin. Eubolo thought he looked more like a demonic Viking than a Norman swordsman.

'Now, let me see what you have learned…if aught!' The barrel chest filled with laughter which rang out around the high walls of the castle tilt-yard. There was a sudden rush to collect a weapon from the trestle which had been laid out for the occasion with a large variety of swords glinting in the pale sunlight. This was the first time they would handle a real weapon. Eubolo and the other pages were being given a glimpse of the future with this doughty warrior, although it would be some years before they would be allowed to use a real sword, so this chance was not to be ignored, and he sprinted to the trestle to choose a sword. He picked up and tested a few before choosing a rusted and pitted old one. The elderly crusader watched as the young squires all began to wield their swords for balance. He noted the sudden change in one slim young squire's face as he realised that the appearance of the rusty old blade belied its true worth. It was an old ploy the master swordsman used in teaching proud young nobles – not all the finest weapons glittered and shone.

'Come, young sirrahs, you have seen the weapons which one day will serve you both on the field of battle and in the tourney. Today, however, you will be showing me your progress with the wooden copies. Your time as pages is quickly coming to an end and on entering my domain you will be exercising, riding and practising weaponry until you ache in more muscles than you knew your body possessed.' He grinned and his yellowed teeth looked gruesome in his huge, hairy face. 'None of your capering nonsense with Master Strongarm, on that you have my word.

'So! Let me see what you have learned over the past weeks. In squads of four at each corner of the square let me see your woeful efforts.'

He called four names and the rest watched carefully, for it was useful to learn both the good and bad moves so that when their turn came they could eradicate the latter. When Eubolo's name was called he wielded his rusty sword with a style and used moves the old 'Master Strongarm' recognised.

'Where did you learn such moves, young LeStrange?'

'One of my father's captains, master!'

'And had your father's captain been on a crusade?'

'Indeed on the Eighth Crusade – with the king.' He stopped, then stammered, 'That is, before he was the king and when he was known as the Lord Edward.'

'So you knew the worth of that old blade?'

'It was light and well balanced and would be a worthy weapon if sharpened and cleaned.'

'Then, young LeStrange, that is what you will do, for I see the makings of a good swordsman if you continue in like vein necessary to the good knight I will make you!' He turned. 'And as to the rest of you, practice, practice and more practice. The harder your lessons are within these walls the easier will be your task on the field of battle.' The old man noted some envious glances cast in the direction of the young Marcher lordling. He would have to watch out for that young man's welfare, for he had undoubted talent. But he was also aware of easily aroused jealousy within this group of young squires. Some would make knights who would honour the code of chivalry. Some would not!

Over the coming years, Eubolo learned the knightly skills. His strength and prowess grew daily. He relished the long hours at the quintain, which also involved riding the powerful destriers, for horses had been part of his upbringing. However, some of the squires proved more adept in the saddle, whilst the quintain frequently became the downfall of many unsuspecting novices, causing much ribaldry among the older squires who wagered amongst themselves on the daily outcome of the tilt-yard.

Meanwhile, the fears held by Maud LeStrange about the impending war in Scotland were to prove well founded. Her husband John, who had also seen action in Gascony as well as frequent action in Wales, also voiced his concerns.

'We are merely pawns in the king's war games. He moves us around the board as he sees fit. It will prove a costly and dangerous strategy given the distance to service an army.'

Maud wished the king's game would not always involve the

LeStrange family who had faithfully served the Plantagenet monarchs, even the treacherous King John, for there was no LeStrange name penned on the Magna Carta. If only women were allowed to rule, wars would be a rarity not the norm. Sadly, women not only bore the pain of childbirth but the even greater pain of loss in the aftermath of battle. But Maud could only rail against the world in private or when talking to other women, for she knew she was powerless to change the course of men and kings. So she busied herself with matters she could control and became reconciled to the troubled times in which she lived.

CHAPTER V

'So the fox and the lion have done England proud! Surrey has restored English pride and the king's honour with a victory at Falkirk!' Thomas of Lancaster stood reading the stained missive. 'I tell you, Harclay, I never thought old Surrey still had it in him!'

Andrew Harclay grinned. 'Aye! Old Warenne has lost none of his soldiering prowess.'

'My uncle will be well pleased and with this victory in Scotland and his forthcoming marriage to the French princess – the omens bode well for the House of Plantagenet.'

Thomas moved to look out over the great castle ramparts. This visit to his wife's mother had at first irked him as he had had to leave the lusty Yolanda at Grosmont but now…

'You know, Harclay, when Pontefract becomes mine I have plans to make significant changes. De Lacy has spent virtually nothing on comforts and has let many repairs go unattended.'

Harclay rubbed his prickly chin as he replied, 'Well, Lincoln has been kept somewhat busy by the king and, as we all know, even the best of stewards fail to achieve the same standards as their patrons.'

Lancaster nodded. 'There's truth in that, I suppose; nonetheless I promise you many changes. Pontefract has been a castle I have always coveted and in my hands it will rival any in England, Wales or France!'

The two men chuckled, neither hearing the entrance of the earl's wife, Alice. As daughter to the Earl of Lincoln the words had cut deep but she bit her lip to stop any rebuff. She had learned that her husband's vindictiveness and spite were frequently vented on those that served her, knowing the distress it caused.

It was Harclay that first became aware of her presence. He cleared his throat and murmured, 'Good morrow, lady.'

Thomas's expression immediately darkened. What was it about this chit of a girl that so irritated him? Maybe it was due to the fact she had failed to conceive as a result of his manhood failing him whenever he visited her bed.

Thomas was completely unaware that Matty's ancient skills had been used to protect the life of her mistress. Matty had left her family home near Pendle simply to escape the family's association with the ancient arts and vowed never to use them. She had wrestled with her own conscience, but the love of her lady was stronger than her own misgivings. To protect Alice's life she had placed a charm in the mattress which ensured she would never again be troubled by her husband's lust and Thomas never knew why his virility failed him in his marriage bed, a fact which added fuel to his antagonism towards his wife.

Upon their return to Grosmont he quickly renewed his amorous relationship with Yolanda. This in no way seemed to affect the young countess. Alice appeared aloof, almost untouchable, and even the many slights and affronts her husband inflicted on her failed to ruffle her calm countenance. Whatever sarcastic insults he used against her, for he had a large coffer of spite, were all to no avail. He failed to realise what it cost Alice to endure her position. It was now common knowledge that Yolanda was his mistress and she flaunted the fact in Alice's face without any redress from Thomas.

Many of his courtiers would, if given a chance, have been just as discourteous, but Alice had also gained many supporters within the household who championed her cause, for the countess, unlike her husband, both knew and cared about their servants. She knew many by name and looked to their welfare in her quiet, unassuming manner. A growing number of pages and squires also held their lady in high regard not for being the daughter of an earl and married to another, but for her own qualities. To them, Alice de Lacy was the epitome of a young noblewoman, devout, compassionate, elegant, and a fine horsewoman, coupled with the fact she was well read and knowledgeable in art and music. The division of loyalty sometimes erupted into actual fights among the pages and squires; this in turn led to some deep-seated rivalries which would continue far into adulthood.

To one of the household this state of affairs caused nothing but amusement. Yolanda Artois was well aware of how her status caused tongues to wag and sides to be taken, but her hold on Thomas was gaining daily. She indulged his physical appetites and desires, she scoffed at her priest when he warned of hellfire and damnation. Her pert response? 'Well, Holy Father, has anyone ever returned from the grave to support your preachings?'

The poor cleric had made the sign of the cross and left abruptly, muttering of blasphemy. He feared for this generation with all their shortcomings and sinful desires and prayed for the knowledge and the strength to counter such sins.

In August, the king's surviving daughter, Eleanor, had died. Her husband, the Count of Bar, was a prisoner of King Philip of France and she had returned to England earlier that year. Her death added another member of the royal family to the list of those who had been laid to rest in Westminster Abbey. Alice sighed; yet another funeral and the hypocritical pretence such ceremonies entailed. However, it would mean she would meet up with her mother and also see Henry, her brother-in-law, who had also become a father that year. His marriage to Maud Chaworth the previous year had been a less ostentatious ceremony than had been her own, but had proved more fruitful.

Once again she would make the journey to London and witness the stark divide between the rich and poor of the country. It was a situation which moved Alice every time she witnessed the starving, ragged peasants along the route, or in the streets and alleys of London itself – from squalid, putrid-smelling districts filled with raucous sounds and scenes of utter depredation to pleasant parks and sumptuous houses with palaces full of grace, elegance and wealth. Her own father owned one of the most prestigious properties in the capital, the Savoy Palace.

Life was full of incongruities. She had long since learned that the wider world was far beyond anything she was able to change. However, Alice always tried to make sure that wherever and whenever possible the households that came under her jurisdiction were well managed, with the welfare of tenants, servants, squires and pages her priority. She had learned this valuable lesson from her father, who always maintained that a well-run, well-organised household was a happy one, where everyone both knew what was expected of them and what their expectations were in return. The same rules also applied to an army, in fact even more so, given that there were so many changes of men who served for their obligatory forty days and had to mix with seasoned mercenary or career soldiers.

The forthcoming occasion called for Alice to choose a wardrobe and jewels, and also to choose gifts for her mother and of course Henry's new-born daughter. Matty often wondered whether her mistress wished she had a child of her own, but nothing was ever spoken between them on the subject.

The winter winds had dropped and a watery sun lit the large chamber in the Savoy Palace. Henry de Lacy stood warming his fingers before the huge, roaring fire. 'I swear my blood has turned to ice, for my fingers feel like spiteful knaves.'

'My dearest husband, you have not stopped complaining since your return to England. This is a new facet to your character and one which I wish you had left in Gascony!' Margaret Longespee frowned as she spoke, which highlighted the ravages the years had marked on her once handsome features.

Alice watched her parents and studied them as if they were strangers. The ageing couple looked like complete opposites of a spectrum. Henry, grossly overweight with great chawls of fat around his chin and neck; Margaret, tall and gaunt with an imperious countenance, although Alice knew this was now mainly due to her short-sightedness. They were her only real defences against her husband's more openly aggressive behaviour towards her. The question she often found herself dwelling on these days was quite simply, what would her life be without them?

The ageing countess turned towards her daughter. 'I swear you have grown taller since we last met and still no sign of a child!' Alice moved away from her mother's line of vision behind a large, high-backed chair.

'Tush, tush! My dear, do not start laying blame on Alice, especially at this time of festivities and mirth. Such matters are in the hands of God!'

Margaret's face tightened and Henry failed to hear her muttered retort, 'More like in the lust of men!'

Although Thomas was amongst the throng at court that Yuletide, Alice managed to experience a time of joy and wellbeing. Henry, her brother-in-law, and his young wife Maud helped to make the most of the entertainment and fun; sometimes it was a little too boisterous in its intensity. The king had paid homage at Canterbury, a custom he had observed since the death of his first wife Eleanor of Castile. Now Margaret of France had stepped into the role as queen and was already pregnant with her first child.

Handsome, kind, gentle Margaret was the complete antithesis of her husband, but their union appeared most compatible and Edward was a much more contented man than of late, at least in his home life. However, the same was certainly not so on the subject of Scotland, the thorn which constantly wounded leaving such a devastating effect, both for the king, his nobles and all the subjects of the realm. Loyal noblemen like Henry de Lacy, the Earls of Warwick, Gloucester and Hereford, and Aymer de Valence, the revered Earl of Pembroke, joined now by the vacuous young Earl of Lancaster. The dangerous challenge from Scotland grew ever more threatening. William Wallace, who had emerged as an effective opponent to Edward's pursuit of Scotland's throne, was a name which threw the king into a rage before ever the final syllable had been uttered.

'I will have that fiend and hang him so high that he will look the devil in the eye!' The roar could be heard throughout the palace, to leave no one in any doubt that the king would never let this 'Great Cause' go until he had wrought his vengeance upon all who opposed him in his quest.

As the king celebrated Yuletide with many of his nobles, one young squire was missing from the Lancastrian retinue. A messenger had brought news that his mother would be at her ancestral home in Warwickshire and Eubolo had gained permission to leave court so that he could visit her.

Maud LeStrange stood holding her fingers before a great, crackling fire and felt happier than she had done for many months. In the place of her birth she could lay the burden of managing a busy, fighting household and all the responsibilities of the feasting and accommodation on her mother's stewards and servants. Her only priority was her wardrobe and waiting for the arrival of her favourite son Eubolo. He was more like her side of the family than any of her other sons. He possessed a merry humour, coupled with charm and grace sadly lacking in the older boys. In fact, Eubolo's appearance bore no resemblance to any of his brothers, who were dark, swarthy and powerfully built with the LeStrange features stamped across their faces. Eubolo was tall and lithe with clean-cut features. He had a disarming smile and curling, light-brown hair. Maud loved him above the others simply because she felt comfortable in his company. They talked freely, sharing the same sense of humour which the other boys lacked, but above all he was kind and considerate. For these qualities he was often teased by the older boys but Eubolo took it all in good part and always managed to turn the tables with his humour and mimicry.

Maud had missed her youngest son when he had left to serve in the Lancastrian household. Notwithstanding, she acknowledged the honour, but a mother looks at more personal emotions when bidding farewell to a child. She stared deep into the red flames and wondered how he had changed since their last meeting. Would he have grown apart from her? Would his new position as squire make him shun his boyish ways? All of these questions would soon be answered and she offered a silent prayer that her son had not stepped beyond his mother's reach.

However, on his arrival all her erstwhile fears faded, for Eubolo's bright, smiling face invaded the chamber and without any sign of embarrassment he swept across the room and hugged his mother in an unashamed show of emotion. Maud's eyes filled with tears of joy. 'How you have grown and how handsome you look!'

That Christmastide was one of the happiest Maud had ever spent. She laughed and danced with her son and the whole place was filled with the true meaning of Christmas. In the morning, they attended Mass and Maud was totally unaware that her son was praying fervently for a pale-eyed lady many leagues away who would also be celebrating her name day. It was the only regret that Eubolo felt throughout that season of feasting and festivities that he was parted from the Countess of Lancaster for he realised that his feelings had grown into something more than admiration.

Even during this period he daily practised his sword drill and tilting at the quintain. He was adamant that he would not fall behind and be left wanting on his return to court. Although he did not tell his mother of certain enmities within the Lancastrian household, he did regale the company with anecdotes and incidents which he knew would amuse. But all too soon the parting hour loomed and Maud felt more personal sadness than she had felt since Eubolo had left some years ago, when he first went to Grosmont.

As usual her son made light of their parting although he too felt more than a tinge of sadness. 'Come now, dearest mother, I am advancing the name of LeStrange and hope to serve my king, my country and my family. You are always in my prayers and we will meet again presently. Father will be at court ere long, you will see!'

Maud smiled through her sadness. 'I pray you are right! God keep you, my dearest boy, you are ever in my heart and my prayers.'

He kissed her cheek, then turned and strode off to mount the black stallion being held by a red-faced groom, as the spirited animal twirled and twisted anxious to be off!

Meantime, Alice de Lacy had been dealt yet another blow by her husband, as he departed for Grosmont to collect more troops for the forthcoming campaign in Scotland. He had assigned her three ladies-in-waiting and their only mission, Alice knew, was to watch her every move and report all to Thomas upon his return. However, for once Margaret Longespee had noted the consternation in her daughter's behaviour at this revelation and when they were alone she challenged her daughter. 'Pray tell me what is amiss.'

When Alice explained to her mother exactly Thomas's reasoning for this new arrangement, Margaret stepped in and without fuss informed her husband about this new move by their son-in-law.

On learning of his wife's concern, the earl called for Luke Lytton. 'Ah, Master Luke, you have been in my daughter's household for a number of years now. Ostensibly it was at my behest?'

'Indeed, my lord earl!' Luke stood watching the ageing earl and noting how time had not proved his friend. He had gained many pounds in weight, his eyes were dark-rimmed, and his shoulders hunched as though against the effects of carrying a great weight.

'My wife informs me that Lancaster has recently ordered three ladies-in-waiting to attend my daughter closely at all times. Pray tell me, what is amiss here?'

Luke moved his weight uncomfortably from foot to foot and began to expand on events which had taken place during the earl's absence. When Luke finally finished, Henry stood rubbing his chin.

'This is a situation which calls for delicate handling. If I openly denounce Lancaster's actions he will undoubtedly take more stringent measures against my daughter.' He turned, then walked towards the window and gazed out over the busy scene below as men-at-arms, archers, horses and armour were all being assembled in readiness for the forthcoming march to Scotland. However, it was a scene lost on Henry, for his mind was lost in deep meditation on his daughter. 'He has also tried to remove you and Mistress Holden from Alice's service – is that not so?'

'Yes, my lord,' Luke murmured.

'Well, we have out-manoeuvred him on that count. Now let us do the same with this situation, without causing my daughter to be placed in an untenable position in the future.'

The two men talked for some considerable time, then the earl dictated three letters and had one of his own messengers summoned. Within an hour of Luke finalising the last letter, a liveried messenger clattered out through the gate on his way to the three unsuspecting households of the luckless young women. Parents were informed that the services of their daughters would now no longer be required and that they would be returning home with a purse of silver for their troubles. The mistake was caused by a misunderstanding and that in no way was any blame attached to any of the women, merely that his wife had, unbeknown to the Earl of Lancaster, already appointed three young women from families who had served the de Lacy family for many generations.

Henry knew that Lancaster would not openly oppose his wishes; he had too much to lose and knowing Henry also had the ear of the king would make it even more pertinent not to appear at odds with his father-in-law. The ageing earl was satisfied with this outcome, but it did not placate the niggling worm of doubt which now gnawed at him – what would happen to Alice when he and her mother were no longer there to protect and look to her wellbeing. A secretary and a waiting woman had no real powers to oppose a Plantagenet earl if such a situation arose again.

But Henry had scant time to dwell on family issues. Scotland was now his priority and once again he began preparations for yet another conflict. At least this one was not overseas, although still too many leagues away for his liking.

The king's determination to bring Scotland to heel was ever at the forefront of his mind and actions. The exchequer was depleted but he ignored the mundane matters of finance. All that mattered to Edward Plantagenet was that he would succeed and he would move heaven and earth to bring it about.

The reality saw a great army march in a colourful, slow procession north, gathering disgruntled troops as they went. In July they were at the castle at Caerlaverock where they began a siege which brought an English victory, feted in ballads that would echo around the courts of Europe for many years. The hero was none other than the Earl of Lincoln, Henry de Lacy, and on his return to Lincoln even the austere Margaret Longespee felt her heart fill with pride. Age it appeared had not blunted her husband's fighting prowess.

As he described the events, she could only imagine the spectacle that must have surrounded the castle, where banners and pennons of every hue flapped and danced in the wind, with the great warhorses thundering across the Scottish landscape. She could almost hear the shouts and screams of the wounded men and animals on both sides filling air pervaded with the smell of death.

The contingent of knights and men-at-arms hailed from every corner of England and the Welsh Marches, names she recognised and a few she did not, but her husband had carried their badges of honour into the fray and been victorious, which was all that mattered, for Margaret Longespee was a proud noblewoman.

Meanwhile, Henry de Lacy stood with a deep frown etched on his craggy features. Margaret stopped her stitching. 'What prompts such a pensive mood?'

He turned and looked at his wife before answering slowly, 'I fear the king has misjudged the mood of his nobles. They have no real appetite for this Scottish conflict and until he listens to reason over the encroachment of the forests he will be hard pressed to raise enough troops for this fresh campaign.'

'Surely he must be aware of the situation?'

Henry smiled wryly. 'He hears exactly what he wishes to hear and is deaf to all else. Oh, for certain he set in motion the perambulation of the forests, which will help, but I fear not with any great haste.' He moved from the window and came to sit before his wife in a heavy-backed chair. 'The old order is changing, there are but few of us left and the younger generation do not...' he hesitated before continuing, '...hold the same attitude towards the king's ideals.'

Margaret put down her needle. 'Are you including your son-in-law?'

'Indeed I am, my dear, together with Hereford, Warwick and Gloucester who have only recently inherited their titles. We are in sore need of men such as Edmund, the king's brother, and Burnell whose shrewd brain and easy charm served the king's cause so efficiently and loyally. I fear things could go badly wrong.'

'And where does Carrick stand in this?'

'Ah!' The frown returned. 'At present we have three guardians in Scotland, Carrick, Comyn and Bishop Lamberton. The latter was appointed not only for his position in the Church, but also to be a buffer between Comyn and Carrick, who most certainly will never agree on anything!'

Margaret watched her husband's face carefully. 'Therefore you foresee trouble?'

'In a nutshell, I see much trouble – in fact, the whole situation is ready to erupt into chaos.'

Margaret picked up her needlework again and continued screwing her eyes in the effort. 'Then your services are essential to contain such matters.'

He looked over at the figure of his wife. 'Without sufficient men it will be more than difficult, pretty well impossible, I fear!'

'But surely the earls and magnates fund their own cavalry regiments and therefore it is only foot-soldiers you lack? And are they not bound to serve the king for forty days when called on?'

'It sounds so easy when you speak thus. However, if a man is called to serve from, say, Hampshire, how long do you think it will take him to reach Scotland?'

The countess pressed her lips together to stop the retort which was about to spring from her lips. Henry began to pace up and down the chamber.

'Men with no heart for a battle are little more than worthless and we cannot afford such a lack of morale within our ranks. The terrain itself is harsh, there is little or no food to forage, thus leaving hungry troops and horses facing both the enemy and the elements. Men deserted in the winter in droves and, in all honesty, who can blame them? Starvation is as much our enemy as are the Scots.'

'Not an enviable position for you, my dear!'

The earl stopped his march up and down and glowered at his wife. 'No, madam, not an enviable position for anyone.'

'Then you must acquaint the king with the true facts.'

'And face his ire?'

'Better to face it in the confines of a chamber than on a hostile battlefield, surely? If you get the king to discuss this encroachment of the forests…'

Henry interrupted. 'Perambulation of the forests.'

Margaret shrugged her shoulders in annoyance. 'Whatever you name it – that which stands in the way of bringing the king what he most desires at this moment, funds to bring about Scotland's submission to his rule.'

'And how do you propose I do that without igniting the king's rage?'

Margaret studied the man that stood before her. Now well into middle age, he had lost all of his youthful qualities and wore his age not well, for he no longer carried the weight of responsibility with ease, as he had once done.

She rose and walked to the window and gazed out on the busy scene below. 'Grasp the nettle, my lord. Better to receive a little sting now than a mortal blow later, surely?'

They stood together for what seemed like an age, then Henry turned to his wife, his face no longer troubled. 'My good lady, you see straight to the kernel ignoring the shell.' He caught her hand and kissed it. 'Then a sting I must bear for the greater good.'

She looked up into his face where the lines of age marked deep furrows between his bushy brows. 'You were never a coward, Henry, and you will earn the king's gratitude eventually. Have patience – you will see the sooner the king addresses this problem of the forests, the sooner he can forward his own cause.'

Henry suddenly smiled. 'However, it will not fill the royal coffer and war, especially this Scottish venture, sucks it dry.'

'The king will always find a way to fund his ventures, especially where war is concerned. Why not approach the Church? Its chests heave with treasures.'

'Oh, it has refused to send any silver to aid the king.'

'Then it should beware, for the Plantagenet memory is long and vengeful.'

'Well, true as that may be, we will cross one bridge at a time.'

However, it was not to the field of battle Henry was summoned, but to the courts of Rome, as the king ordered him to attend on his behalf to plead the English position in the Scottish wars. Therefore, it was the diplomat's bonnet, not the warrior's helm, that was required on this occasion. Both had been well worn in the service of his king and country. Inevitably it meant a long and tedious journey, accompanied by many saddle sores, through the mud, wet and cold of winter on the roads through Europe.

CHAPTER VI

Grosmont Castle
Spring 1301

The great walls of Grosmont Castle echoed with the sounds of soldiers, mercenaries, knights and their chargers and all their servants, grooms and squires. The clamour of the blacksmiths' hammers rang out in rhythmic, steady beats. Somewhere a piper played a lively marching tune and the shouts of the commanders rose up to the chambers where Alice and Matty stood watching the scene below.

'As soon as they have all gone, we will make ready to go to Clitheroe Castle.' Alice never felt comfortable at Grosmont – it was imposing and far too grand and ostentatious for her simpler tastes. Everything was on such a large scale. The elaborate tapestries, the sumptuous furnishings and the ornate furniture were more on the French style than the plainer English fashion Alice had known in her parents' castles. Only the Savoy Palace in London was more lavish than the countryside castles, but then that was only to be expected, given the position her father held at court.

Matty moved towards her mistress and handed her the warm shawl for the castle draughts were ever chilling even here amongst the luxuries.

'How I wish I could ride out and earn honours and great victories. Reputations can be made on the field of conflict. My father must be so disappointed that neither of my brothers survived to sit beside him on the field of battle.' She looked wryly at her waiting lady. 'Only a mere daughter who cannot even produce an heir to continue with the great family traditions.'

Matty caught the hand of her mistress. 'Oh, that fault is never yours, my lady. Neither is the death of your brothers and I cannot believe that your father has ever felt one single moment of regret for having such a wonderful daughter.'

Alice squeezed Matty's hand. 'You are always my champion and comfort and I give thanks for your presence every day, for what would my life be without you, dearest Matty?'

'Our lives are governed by God but fashioned by men and kings. Therefore we, as mere women, find it difficult sometimes to understand their ways. However, when the king commands we must all obey or suffer the consequences!'

The two women were silent for awhile, then Alice broke the silence. 'Aye! That is nothing but the truth.' Alice smiled at her lady-in-waiting, then said mischievously, 'At least Earl Arrogance will be kept busy for a while at the king's pleasure and vent his tempers towards the Scots!' And the two women smiled at each other in unashamed glee.

Whilst Alice and Matty prepared to leave Grosmont for Clitheroe, the king was facing the very topic that had been on the mind of the Earl of Lincoln before his departure to Rome: the matter of the encroachment of the forests of England and all the animosity that entailed. As the Crown had taken more and more land for the royal hunt over many years, the resentment of those affected had become more vociferous. It was now at the very centre of the failure to recruit men for the army. Landowners had little or no appetite for the king's continuing wars.

It was a fact which the king baulked at accepting as truth. Lack of funds was the prime cause of unpaid soldiers and mercenaries deserting the king's army in droves. During the harsh winter so many had returned home it left those still remaining vulnerable, and ill-fed with scant supplies, given that the scorched earth policy currently offered up no sustenance for men or their animals. The hunger and desertion of so many of his troops were the deadliest enemies that the king faced during that period.

Edward was now prepared to address the problem of the perambulation of the forests or stand to lose everything in what he deemed his 'Great Cause'. Unpalatable as it was it had finally become quite clear that without the goodwill of his subjects his own determination to bring Scotland under his jurisdiction would fail. Ever mindful of his father's disastrous relationship with his barons Edward knew he must swallow his Plantagenet pride to gain the goal he had set himself.

The king called a parliament for the spring, and not a perfunctory one but one which was for men from many walks of life: burgesses, magnates, prelates, earls, nobles and merchants, but Edward was in a mean mood. He hated being forced into acknowledging the powers of his subjects, for he felt that as king his wishes should be paramount. However, he had begun to realise that without the co-operation of his people he would achieve nothing, for taxation, as ever, was always unpopular, and because the Church had failed to provide funds thanks to the constant refusal by his Archbishop of Canterbury, Robert Winchelsea, once again his subjects would bear the burden of the wars with even greater taxation.

The parliament at Lincoln was not an easy one. The question of the perambulation and the charters pertaining to them set the mood, where on both sides neither looked to concede. The king called on his clerics for documents to uphold his claim as he mistrusted the memory of his subjects on the matter of the forest areas. On the other hand, without the concession to his nobles and subjects, he would be in no position to raise further taxes and therefore hamstrung in pursuing his Scottish cause. Backed into a corner the king's mood was as Henry de Lacy had predicted, both black and vicious.

The beleaguered committee, which had been given the unenviable task of judging the rights of both parties, voted in favour of the charters over the Crown, thereby upholding the rights of the commoner over the wishes of the king. The decision caused much discomfort amongst the unfortunate members of the committee, for they were fearful that one day they would be accused of treachery towards the king.

On the king's part, he then ordered that the Magna Carta and the Forest Charter should stand and the perambulation would be put into place, without delay. So on the fourteenth of February 1301 many thousands of acres which had been encroached by the Crown for the royal sport of hunting were finally restored to their former ownership, much to the chagrin of the king.

However, when parliament had complained about the corruption of Walter Langton, urging his dismissal, the king had flown into a fury, suggesting sarcastically that '*everyone should have a crown*'. His minister remained in office, for Edward was not about to concede any further powers. In fact, the outcome of this parliament would remain with the king for the rest of his life as he felt that he had been put under the 'stress of necessity' which had led to the surrendering of what he saw as his hereditary rights.

The move by the king to placate the disgruntled landowners would now remove any further obstacles to the raising of the much-needed taxes, which was set for the autumn. In Canterbury during the spring, ambassadors from France and Scotland were meeting to propose a three-way peace treaty. The king's representatives had strict instructions not to countenance such a treaty, nor in fact to continue with the short truce with Scotland which had held over the winter.

When the news of the death of his cousin, Edmund of Cornwall, reached the king, he travelled to Gloucester to attend the funeral. His mood plummeted even further with this personal loss. But the fates were not all set against the king; in fact with the return of his loyal Earl of Lincoln the news from Rome was nothing if not positive.

Boniface, although not finding in the king's favour on the matters of Gascony and Scotland, had agreed to the Church paying a ten per cent tax for the next three years, of which the king would receive half the profits. Boniface needed the balance of these taxes for his own conflict with Sicily. The king cared little for the reasoning, only that it allowed him to gather more money for his armies. It also gave him a small but significant victory over his Archbishop of Canterbury, Robert Winchelsea, who had adamantly refused to sanction any funds from the Church for the past half decade.

Now the king waited for his son, Prince Edward, to return from Caernarfon where he had been receiving homage from his Welsh subjects in his role as Prince of Wales; these also included the powerful Marcher barons. The ageing king mused over his move to bestow the lands and titles on his heir, much as his own father had done at the prince's age, as he fast approached manhood. The lordship of Chester was also included in this new transferring of power, wealth and titles.

Their reunion took place at Kenilworth Castle where they were joined by Queen Margaret. After a short sojourn the royal party travelled north once more to face their Scottish enemy. The prince was now commander of a considerable force and no longer played a junior role. The king held high hopes that by subduing the Scots with a great victory for his son, it would pave the way for his future role as king.

The plan was to trap the enemy in a two-pronged attack, one army led by the king, the other by his son, leaving the enemy no refuge from their combined onslaught. The fighting force was recruited from landowners both in England, Wales and the Welsh Marches. Their numbers were also swelled by an Irish contingent for the first time in the Scottish campaign.

The prince enjoyed a great success in taking the castles of Ayr and Turnberry without too much opposition. Turnberry was hailed as a significant victory, being the birthplace of the erring Robert Bruce, who in the previous year had been removed as one of the three guardians of Scotland.

However, the king was not advancing with nearly as much speed from his base in Berwick. The densely wooded forests of Selkirk proved a difficult barrier to cross with such a large army of men, horses and equipment. However, by mid August the two armies were within thirty miles of each other.

In early September the progress of the English forces was checked by a Scottish force laying siege to the garrison at Lochmaben at the rear of the prince's forces.

Another enemy of the English now beginning to be felt, by both the king and the prince, was the lack of funds. This meant that the mercenaries and foot-soldiers received no pay, which caused them to desert in great numbers. No matter how many irate letters were sent to the treasury by the king the much-needed funds were often too little too late and the king could only fume in impotent fury. Burnell would never have failed him on such an important matter, of that he felt certain; his former chancellor would have understood the situation all too well and funds would have been sent with alacrity.

When Henry de Lacy wrote to his wife of their exploits, he emphasised the king's utter feelings of desperation and anger and knew she would understand the situation. By October the king realised that their position was now untenable. Lack of troops, provisions and funds would prove too powerful an enemy, and the castles so recently taken were now under siege from the Scots. Ayr and Turnberry had too few men to sustain any long sieges and even the prince's army dwindled with the Irish and unpaid troops disappearing daily.

In Selkirk Forest, the Scots were mustering their forces. As the situation was now too serious for the king not to take decisive action, he needed to use his wits rather than force of arms to defeat his accursed enemy.

As soon as Edward had established himself and his remaining army at Linlithgow he summoned the hated minister Walter Langton to go to France to negotiate terms which would change the balance in Scotland. The king saw the move by Pope Boniface to release the erstwhile king of Scotland, John Baliol, as a calculated action to which an equally calculated response was required. The king always enjoyed a challenge, whether on the field of battle or in the council chamber, and this was a perfect opportunity to fight like with like.

Certain that Philip of France was all talk with no real wish for anything more than posturing for position, Edward waited for his cunning minister to do his work; Walter Langton did not fail his monarch.

The situation in Europe was to have a profound effect on Scotland's future. Philip IV of France had been their ally and had promised aid for their cause. However, the pope, who had ordered the English king to desist from hostilities in Scotland, now found himself in a vulnerable position and tempered his outright condemnation with his own situation very much to the forefront of his actions. Edward played his hand with cunning for he knew that Philip would act out of character if he were to send troops and money to the Scots; therefore all his erstwhile promises to them would count for naught. It would leave the Scots in an unenviable position.

So Edward promised to withdraw from Scotland on the condition that Philip should send his troops to maintain the truce, something he gambled the French king would never do. His gamble proved correct. The great wheel of fortune was beginning to swing back in Edward's favour once again.

With the approaching winter, Edward, already encamped at Linlithgow, moved to Falkirk, where he was joined by his son, the Prince of Wales, together with his young wife Margaret of France, who had recently been delivered of her second son Edmund.

A great tournament was to be held which would serve Edward on three counts. One, it was a clear message to the Scots that he was the conqueror and the memory of the English defeat at Falkirk some years before was blotted from memory. Secondly, it would keep his knights and troops entertained and, thirdly, it would be a celebration for the birth of another son. A further event to add to the English king's satisfaction was the surrender of Robert Bruce, confirmed by a hard-riding messenger from Lochmaben.

CHAPTER VII

Clitheroe Castle
1302

Whilst the majority of England's nobility were in Scotland, the lack of a ruler and his magnates left England in a state of lawlessness. Bands of ruthless robbers roamed the land virtually without check, and honest folk were gripped by fear as they went about their daily business.

However, that Christmastide, there was one place where none of the outside world's troubles penetrated, where a state of comfort, wellbeing and merriment presided. Alice de Lacy celebrated her name day in a state of relaxed enjoyment. Thomas was far away in Scotland and she was beginning to find a role in life which suited her well, that of chatelaine of his castles and estates. She had frequently been regaled by her husband's complaints – how he was served by dolts and incompetent fools and thanks to this mismanagement was losing revenue. Alice now undertook the overseeing of his landholdings and found she was not only perfectly equipped to deal with the majority of outstanding issues but she enjoyed the challenge.

Accompanied by Luke, Alice listened to tenants' complaints. She ruled with a fair and even hand and began to earn the respect of those around her. Notwithstanding, she changed stewards where necessary, promoted efficient servants and moved staff around without many even being aware of their shortcomings. Alice used skills learned from her father: merely by giving a fancy-sounding title and an increase in pay to those affected, which resulted in virtually little or no animosity.

So in this season of goodwill and celebrations Alice could sit back in one of her favourite castles and allow herself some freedom.

Music, feasting and fun were the order of the day. Looking around her, Alice felt secure and almost happy. Matty and Luke Lytton had been joined by a few young squires who had remained to serve their young countess whilst many of the older ones had gone with the earl to Scotland.

Amongst those that remained was the young Eubolo LeStrange. He was proving to be an excellent swordsman and at first resented being left behind. However, he now saw his duty was to serve his lady and day by day Eubolo fell under the gentle spell of Alice de Lacy.

In the hunting field Alice was a fearless rider, but Eubolo was touched by the fact that her concern for a clean kill was paramount and that the welfare of the hawks and hounds was of the utmost importance. How unlike Earl Thomas and his close group of companions, for the bloodier and more brutal the kill, the more enjoyment they appeared to gain from the sport.

Cockfighting Alice allowed. Bear-baiting she did not! In fact, Alice had saved a bear from certain death when she was very young and still kept it as a pet.

Throughout the season of Yuletide there were games which brought gales of laughter from both those who played and those that watched. The company danced to melodic, tuneful strains of music and there was also entertainment from a young troubadour whose sweet voice serenaded the company with ballads of love and brave deeds of valour which included the ballad of Caerlaverock.

It had been an eventful time for Matty Holden too, for she had finally accepted the attentions of Luke Lytton. He had promised to be content with playing a subservient role in her life as long as they were together. It was a condition she could scarcely refuse. Being a widow had been a difficult period in her life for she had loved her husband Hugh with a passion. With Luke, her relationship was much gentler, more undemanding, and one she was now prepared to give a chance.

For her young mistress Alice, it was another cause for celebration, but it did strike a note of fear into her heart, for without Matty's constant help and unstinting affection she felt she would never be able to survive. It also caused a pang of envy within her breast for Alice had never felt true love. She found herself musing on the condition which caused poets to write reams of verse and songsters to sing countless ballads in praise of love. What would it be like to have one's heart beat faster at a chance meeting, or to receive a love token? She could only muse and wonder.

All too soon the festivities ended and the company made arrangements to return to Grosmont where the earl would soon appear and the old regime would resume, much to the chagrin of one and all. However, one young woman received the news with relief. Yolanda Artois had hated every minute of Thomas's absence. She enjoyed her position as his mistress whilst in his company, but left to her own devices Yolanda became bored and truculent. Hearing the news of his imminent return raised her spirits, and she began to order new clothes and jewels to adorn herself, for she knew that absence did not always work in favour of the one left behind.

However, Thomas's return to Grosmont was but a brief visit as he was expected to attend the king on his travels from Scotland. His reunion with his wife was a cool, matter-of-fact greeting, whereas with Yolanda it was the complete opposite, a re-ignition all their carnal appetites as they resumed their passionate, scandalous affair. When Alice learned that the hated mistress would also be accompanying them she flatly refused to go and made hasty arrangements to go to Canford and visit her mother. This was to begin a pattern of separation which would mark the future relationship of the Earl and Countess of Lancaster. The two parties would live as far apart from each other as possible and only meet when duty dictated.

In one instance only was the earl quite ready to accede to Alice and her capabilities and that was in the management of his estates. He could not deny revenues had risen considerably since Alice had taken the reins and he saw no earthly reason why their personal differences should interfere with this arrangement. So the Lancastrian household split into two factions, the greater number attending the earl whilst a smaller number were attached to the countess. The arrangement happened almost imperceptibly and caused no great disruption.

Developing events in Europe during 1302 added to the English king's position of power in Scotland. Edward and Philip IV continued their long-standing dispute which involved not only the Scottish wars but also the question of suzerainty of Gascony, a persistent source of animosity between the two kings. Although Edward had ostensibly won his claim to the Gascon lands on the field of battle the French king disputed English rights in the council chamber. However, in the summer of that year, the people of Flanders openly revolted against French rule, causing Philip to send troops and cavalry to quell the uprising. They were, however, repelled by armed townspeople who against all odds won a resounding victory, killing many important lords. Amongst their numbers was one of France's chief ministers, Pierre Flote. So much wealth was claimed by the victors that day that it was dubbed the 'Battle of the Golden Spurs' and would be celebrated for centuries to come.

Adding to the French king's woes, a vicious quarrel broke out between Philip and Pope Boniface over the perceived mistreatment of a French bishop. With such catastrophes piling up for Edward's old adversary, he was enjoying this turn of events, which again affected Scotland's place in the courts of Europe. Boniface quickly changed his stance, even writing to one of Scotland's premier bishops, Robert Wishart, admonishing him for condoning and encouraging resistance against the English king. Whilst matters festered on the Continent, Edward was able to relax for a while hunting and enjoying family pursuits. He could quite happily leave all the wrangling to act as a further weapon in his 'Great Cause'.

Philip was now most anxious to treat with Edward. The promised aid for Scotland melted like winter snow.

In the last days of autumn of that year Edward did in fact enter into a treaty with France, but of Scotland there was no mention. It left Edward in the position he had wished for, to be free to pursue his claim on Scotland unhindered by either Rome or France.

However, although the king now had some funds for his campaigns across the border, there was not nearly sufficient to warrant complacency. Provisions, livestock and men were still of paramount importance, and keeping the troops supplied, especially in winter, invariably had to be done by sea.

Although Scotland had been abandoned by both the pope and the French, it served only to harden their resolve to push the English back across the border. Castles at Linlithgow and Selkirk once again came under Scottish attacks. Early in the New Year, the former held but Selkirk fell. As the year progressed further bad news arrived when one of Edward's chief ministers in Scotland, Sir Ralph Manton, was attacked and slain near to Roslin. Manton, known as the king's paymaster, was a significant loss. The battle had been one of the bloodiest and most hard-fought of the whole campaign up to then.

The English king's rage knew no bounds. He was now determined to bring about a satisfactory conclusion to this war and ordered every available man from every corner of his kingdom including Ireland, Wales and the north to hold themselves in readiness for a final confrontation with his hated adversary. Every debt, every penny Edward could call on to fill his coffers was diligently pursued. Urgency and determination were the order to his commanders and all knew if they did not respond to their monarch's demands his wrath would be felt not only by them but their families too!

Edward turned to his engineers in whom he now placed his trust. His aim was to strike deep into the heartlands of his most aggressive opponent, the Comyns, and his intention was to attack from a new position for which the skills of his engineers was vital. They were ordered to construct a pontoon bridge, thus enabling Edward to land his men in the unguarded areas along the Forth. A great fleet made ready to carry the supply of troops, horses and knights to the campaign sites and the men of Norfolk were recruited in order to build the bridge.

For all the great plans and urgent building, these pontoons were never used, but the scheme pointed to the fervour of the king's purpose in bringing all to bear in his attempt to defeat his accursed adversary, the Scots.

For the womenfolk of both nations, there was also a struggle, a struggle for their very existence. Without men to till the land and harvest the crops families were left to starve. It was a time when Alice de Lacy set up small infirmaries wherever she could under the guidance of Ralph the old physician. Matty too distilled herbs and unctions to aid the sick and injured.

Whilst Alice was kept busy with matters of the estates and the ever-growing numbers of sick and starving flocking to the gates of the castles within her jurisdiction, her husband, Thomas of Lancaster, was gaining a reputation for bluff and bluster, but his efforts ended with little or no positive results. This fact did not escape the notice of both the king and his councillors, and among their numbers was none other than Henry de Lacy, Lancaster's father-in-law.

However, the English king, once more beleaguered by lack of funds, men and provisions, still managed to push the Scots to the brink of defeat, and when finally the Comyn family realised that there was no alternative, they surrendered in the first months of 1303. Whatever Edward felt personally about his victory, the knightly values he still held, albeit hidden at times, ensured that he acknowledged and proffered the respect that the dour Scots had earned over the passing years of almost continual fighting. Now none but Stirling Castle remained defiant and Edward brought all his might against that impregnable stronghold. Great trebuchets were wheeled into place and lead stripped from every available church, abbey and building to feed the great catapults. During more than two months of constant bombardment, the engineers and carpenters constructed an even bigger machine, which they dubbed 'The Warwolf'.

Edward was so thrilled by this achievement that even after the castle had finally surrendered, he insisted on watching the enormous machine in action. The whole siege had been a spectacle on a scale previously unheard of, where even 'Greek Fire' had been used, something that Edward had seen when he had been on crusade many years before.

Once again the valour of the Scottish defenders went without acknowledgment, as they had only been accorded their lives after agreeing to walk barefoot in the guise of penitents in sackcloth and ashes. With the surrender of Stirling Castle there was left just one final goal against the Scots, the capture of William Wallace, who had never sworn fealty to Edward and had vowed to die before ever doing so. To the eternal shame of the Scots, Wallace was eventually betrayed by one of his own people in August 1305.

The bloody and brutal end to such a brave and courageous warrior marked a change in many of those who watched the gruesome spectacle of his bloody execution. But Edward Plantagenet now felt he could finally draw a line under a period that had caused him so many sleepless nights, and he rejoiced and gave thanks to God for allowing him to live to see this day, little knowing that even with Wallace's death his wars in Scotland were not at an end.

CHAPTER VIII

1305

With Comyn's surrender and Wallace's death, the treaty with Scotland enabled Edward to enjoy a brief period of respite, for age was now sitting more heavily upon the royal shoulders. The state of outlawry which had pervaded England during his prolonged absences in the north was now being addressed by newly appointed officials.

Scottish law and order were also of paramount importance and Edward vowed not to repeat mistakes made by previous appointments in Scotland. Robert Bruce's loyalty was rewarded as were a number of others, but only a handful of English nobles and official were amongst the appointees.

However, just as Edward was getting to grips with long-outstanding issues in England, arising from his time spent in the field of conflict, a more personal argument boiled over between the royal father and son. The Prince of Wales had by all accounts argued with the unpopular Bishop of Coventry and Lichfield, Walter Langton, an argument which the king was not going to ignore. To throw insults at one of the king's chief ministers was not to be condoned – not even by his own son, however trivial the issue may or may not have been.

The king had throughout his life been a good judge of men, a fact which had served him well over his long years on the throne. Now his son had reached his majority, his many shortcomings were becoming increasingly more apparent to his father. Sadly, not only his son's lack of kingly qualities but his nephew, Thomas of Lancaster, had also inherited precious few, if any, of the many virtues of his late brother Edmund, and the king could only lament that fact. The old order was passing and the new left wanting.

In high dudgeon, the king sent the prince from his presence and for many weeks refused any moves to become reconciled. It left a contrite prince trailing after his father like some discarded puppy. Only his constant companion Piers Gaveston kept him amused. Even the pleas by Margaret the queen were left unheeded, much to her disappointment.

As in many family quarrels, tempers cooled and a royal reconciliation was finally achieved in October. The prince was so relieved he threw a great feast in honour of his father. Amongst those that were in attendance were the Earl of Lancaster and his wife, Countess Alice de Lacy.

Alice felt like an observer who was somehow not part of the assembly. She watched the various factions manœuvre around the court, sometimes huddled in groups. Her husband Thomas led the rowdiest and the most drunken of them all.

After the feasting, as the trestle tables were moved back to allow the entertainment to proceed, the elegant figure of Piers Gaveston moved to Alice's side. 'You are looking well, my lady!'

Alice smiled. 'Pray have a care, for I espy my husband watching you! It would achieve nothing to upset him for no reason other than to play your game of mischief, my lord.' The dark, handsome face broke into a smile and he leaned forward.

'Lady Alice, I promise I offer you no hurt, nor would I bring down your husband's displeasure. However, pray do not deny me some small morsel of fun, for the churlish dolt to whom you are married needs belittling from time to time, don't you agree? We are alike, you and I.'

At his words, Alice turned and a look of sheer incredulity spread across her face, her normal composure slipping for an instant. 'You and I, my lord Gaveston, have absolutely nothing in common either by gender or by situation.'

The dark eyebrows rose at her words. Then his voice dropped almost to a whisper. 'We have been cast in roles we may not have chosen for ourselves; therefore you and I play the roles we were given and we play them as if our lives depend upon it!' And he hesitated before continuing, 'As in fact they do!'

Before Alice could say anything further the Prince of Wales sauntered across to stand beside his friend. 'Come now, Piers, you will provoke my cousin's anger at monopolising his wife's company.'

'I am merely acquainting the Lady Alice with the truth of events in Scotland.' The dark eyes twinkled with amusement as he spoke.

The prince, with lowered voice, whispered, 'Do not believe all the boastful claims of my cousin.' And the two inseparable companions moved back to where the rest of their group were chatting and laughing. Alice was aware that her husband watched her with an expression of undisguised rage. She turned and noted that her father and the king were talking in hushed tones, but as the topic was obviously confidential she moved away. The mood of the evening was mainly of merriment and the jesters and balladeers entertained the throng throughout.

Matters in Scotland were in hand, the queen pregnant with their third child, and apart from the ever-constant wrangling with the Archbishop of Canterbury, Robert Winchelsea, Edward felt more at ease than he had done for some considerable time. He had even contemplated going on a crusade, something he had vowed to do years previously. However, this period of comparative calm lasted but a few short months, for during 1306 Scotland's cauldron of trouble once more boiled over.

Such was the seriousness of events that the king was brought to the very edge of sanity. Bruce's crime was so heinous that when Edward first learned of it he held the news in total disbelief. Robert Bruce, the Earl of Carrick, who had played such a significant part in subduing his fellow-countrymen, had been appointed with John Comyn to organise Scotland's leaders and head a council, even though the two men had a long-standing quarrel. This quarrel then apparently erupted into violent argument, which had resulted in John Comyn's death. The crime was made even worse as the location of the murder was within the church of Greyfriars in Dumfries.

Edward was so incensed that his physicians feared for his life. He marched around his chamber shattering goblets, smashing furniture and swearing so vehemently that spittle flew from his mouth at every word.

'This damned, cursed land is bedevilled by traitors and men of treachery. I vow I will not be thwarted by such acts of desecration. Scotland is a leprous sore and Bruce will be brought to trial for his actions. God has laid his curse upon those that oppose me. Divine retribution will prevail.'

Even the gentle Margaret of France kept to her chamber until the king's mood began to subside, but that took many days. The effects on Edward were all too obvious, and when his rage subsided so did his health.

Agents were ordered north to discover how this murder affected the situation along the Scottish and the northern borders. Edward and his councillors were in no doubt that the whole matter of sovereignty over Scotland was about to erupt once more as Robert Bruce, on the death of his father, could legitimately lay claim to the throne of Scotland.

They were not wrong in their assumptions, for Robert Bruce, Earl of Carrick, had been crowned king of Scotland only days after Red Comyn's death. This final piece of news acted like a physical blow to Edward. Henry de Lacy, who had known the king all his life, felt a cold cramp of fear clutch in his stomach and wondered how this incident would affect his sovereign's health. The crown would not be in such sure hands when the Prince of Wales inherited the throne, and how would that serve England? However, such matters were for another day. Whilst Edward still ruled, Henry stood firm in his service but he looked to the future with uncertainty.

The king made arrangements to travel to Scotland but his progress was fearfully slow. As the once vigorous king was now forced to journey by litter, it did little for his temper. Finally, admitting that he was unfit to travel further, Edward ordered Aymer de Valence, the Earl of Pembroke, north to take command. Responsibility would also fall on the Prince of Wales, who had only recently been granted lands in Gascony, a sign his father acknowledged his own failing health.

The appetite for yet another war in Scotland was faltering. To whip up the flagging enthusiasm amongst the younger members of the nobility, Edward initiated a ceremony whereby over three hundred noblemen would become knights. The ceremony, which was to be held at Westminster, would become known as 'The Feast of the Swans'.

The great pageant was followed by a ceremony whereby three hundred, mostly young men, were knighted. Although Edward's body was fast failing him his wits were as sharp as ever. He judged this an act which would unite his nobles and their followers in serving his son and heir, the Prince of Wales.

The earls, barons and bannerets that were not already in Scotland came dressed in their finest garments to the celebration, which was enjoyed by many of the young squires whose years of dedication, hard work and practice in feats of weaponry and horsemanship would all result in their ultimate goal – a knighthood. From all corners of the realm they came and Henry de Lacy stood beside his daughter on the steps of the Great Hall to watch the spectacle, but Henry's concern was for the king whose health he knew was failing fast. Would this be his last great state occasion? Only time would tell, but the Earl of Lincoln felt a deep sadness catch his heart. He had served the greatest king in Christendom since the legendary Arthur himself. He knew the son was cast from a different mould. Nevertheless, as Earl of Lincoln, he had sworn to serve the Crown and in this capacity he would continue to do just that, for his oath was his bond.

Alice sensed her father's sombre mood. 'You have misgivings, papa?'

Henry smiled. How changed was his daughter nowadays from the nervous girl who had married into the royal family so long ago. The girl was now a self-contained young woman, elegant, dignified and gracious. She studied the scene before them, noting the excited young squires who on the morrow would be knighted.

'Look, all the noble houses of England!' she exclaimed softly.

Henry squeezed her hand. 'The king has played his cards well, methinks! By this single act he is uniting the nobility by honouring their young sons and a few ancient ones as well,' he said, chuckling as he spied Roger Mortimer of Chirk, who had long passed his youth, but was only now being knighted with his nephew, also named Roger, who was the heir to the Marcher lands at Wigmore and yet to reach his majority.

The Great Hall at Westminster rang with voices and laughter, music and mummery. The trestle tables groaned under the weight of the many dishes of venison, suckling pigs, geese, ducks, capons, all dressed with skill and ingenuity. Trenchers were filled to overflowing with rich, spiced sauces. Pies of every shape and design were carried in to the waiting guests. Heaped dishes of vegetables, fruit and nuts added colour and variety to the fare. On the king's table sat the magnificent dishes of dressed swans with all their plumage artistically replaced to give diners the impression that they swam across the table.

A thousand candles lit the high, grey walls which had been decked lavishly with greenery. Fresh, sweet-smelling rushes scattered that morning were quickly being crushed beneath so many feet. Wine and ale flowed in copious quantity and both Alice and her father noted the vast amounts of wine being consumed by Thomas of Lancaster, a fact which had not escaped the sharp gaze of Piers Gaveston. An arched eyebrow indicated his observation.

Alice leaned closer to her father and whispered, 'My husband appears to be enjoying the king's wine!' Henry's answer was a simple grunt of disapproval. Thomas of Lancaster was a sore disappointment to the earl. Youthful excesses were excusable, but Thomas had reached maturity some time since and his behaviour, instead of improving, was deteriorating noticeably at every encounter.

Eventually when the king and his guests had eaten and drunk their fill, the trestle tables were quickly moved to the sides of the hall and the musicians and dancers entertained the throng. The prince's own musician, Richard the Rhymer, gave a beautiful rendering of an ancient ballad which drew thunderous applause.

Music was one of the greatest pleasures in Alice's life and she sat entranced. Her rapt expression was noted by a young squire who sat with his family. Eubolo LeStrange was both proud and saddened by the occasion. He knew his mother was overwhelmed by all the high-born ladies in their fashionable garments and dazzling jewellery and that his father felt uncomfortable in his new robes, but his heart was with the pale-eyed young countess who sat at the top table next to her distinguished father and dissolute husband. How many nights had he lain awake wrestling with the knowledge that he had fallen hopelessly in love with his patron's wife? It was a love doomed to failure, doomed to be buried deep within his heart for all time. Death would be his reward if ever the truth reached the light of day; all knew Thomas Plantagenet, Earl of Lancaster, to be a vicious, brutal man, who would quickly dispatch anyone who stood in his way. Although there was no love lost betwixt him and his wife, she was looked upon as his chattel and he could do with her as he wished. Eubolo knew that Alice's father had made it clear that his son-in-law's treatment of his daughter was under scrutiny and this for the time being would afford Alice more protection than she realised.

But Eubolo had witnessed some of the cruel behaviour that

Thomas had meted out to his wife. He had lashed out once at her little hawk and it was only the quick action of her falconer Gilbert that had saved the little merlin. The wound he had received was deep and took many weeks to heal. There had also been the occasion when Thomas had snatched Alice's little dog from her lap, thrown it into the bear pit and laughed as the little dog had been ripped to shreds before his mistress's distraught gaze. He had threatened to have Alice's horse destroyed because it had outjumped his in the hunting field. So many wicked and hurtful incidents ran through his mind.

When he had been assigned to Alice's retinue, he had done everything in his power to serve her and try to show his devotion whenever and wherever he could, without bringing any notice to his acts of thoughtfulness. If Alice had not made any comment, her lady-in-waiting Matty Holden had been all too aware of the young squire's actions. She had even taken him aside and warned him that although his kindness was commendable he could put their mistress in great danger. However, they both agreed that to watch over the Lady Alice was their prime role in life and they and a few others who were also devoted to the quiet, young noblewoman devised a secret signal when they perceived any impending dangers.

Eubolo became aware of his mother pulling at his sleeve. 'Pray tell me, where were your thoughts?'

'Oh, just on the morrow.' He blushed at the lie and hoped she had not seen.

Maude LeStrange did not notice her son's blushes for she was far too busy watching the great and powerful lords with their wives who sat in the vast hall. Many families she knew, especially among the Marcher barons. The Mortimers, the De Greys, the Earl of Gloucester, the handsome Ralph Monthermer, who held the title until his eldest stepson came of age. Then there were the Earls of Hereford and Warwick, neither of whom Maud felt were men she would trust. The same applied to the Despencers, father and son; she knew there was bad blood between them and the Mortimers and for all their reputation she knew whom she would have at her husband's side in a field of battle and it most certainly was not the Despencers. Maud's gaze also fell upon the handsome figure of the Prince of Wales with his companion, the dark, good-looking Gascon.

'Night and day!' she murmured.

Eubolo leaned closer. 'Did you speak, mama?'

'Take no count of me, my dear, just an old woman's prating.'

Eubolo grinned. 'Never old, mama, never old.'

She punched him playfully on the arm. But Maud felt uneasy at her observations that night. The king and queen left quite early in the evening's celebrations leaving the prince to continue as host. However, it was the Gascon who had taken over the role, much to the chagrin of Thomas of Lancaster and many the other earls, who felt that the foreigner was overstepping his role as companion.

Maud had noted too the glowering expression of the Earl of Surrey, John de Warenne. She saw in the midst of the festivities there were matters festering to which she was not party. Nonetheless, they might well have future connotations which could affect the lives of her beloved sons, especially Eubolo who served in the household of Lancaster. One thing Maud had noted, the Countess of Lancaster was in every sense of the word a lady. Composed, gracious and polite, Alice de Lacy looked regal in her dark-green surcote and russet kirtle. Her headdress was of filigree gold with tiny topaz gems, which twinkled and danced with every movement of her head. Her high cheekbones, straight nose and pale-grey eyes could never be called beautiful, but there was an appealing quality about Alice which defied description. The white barbette and crespine hid the thick, rich-brown tresses, but Maud had caught a glimpse of a stray curl which had escaped their confines. Yes, the Countess of Lancaster looked as though she had an engaging manner, but as to her husband! Maud made a note to question Eubolo further on that man's character when they were next alone. As for her own impressions she judged him to be a bully.

During the next day's ceremony, Henry de Lacy stood once again at the side of his daughter. He noted the faraway look in her eyes and guessed her thoughts were not with the events of the day. Exactly what Alice had on her mind he tried to find out by saying, 'I would pay a silver penny for your thoughts.'

Dragged back to the present, Alice smiled sadly at her father. 'You would be wasting your silver, I fear!' she whispered. Further speech was lost as the fanfare for the start of the knighting ceremony began.

Henry had much on his mind but his daughter's future bothered him greatly. The prestigious marriage was sour, and he knew that he was to blame for choosing her husband. His wife Margaret, who had not journeyed to London due to a bout of ill health, had been right when she had written to tell him of events she had noted on her last visit to her daughter, many months before. There was a rift between Thomas and Alice which appeared to grow wider as each day passed. The relationship needed to be watched carefully, and Henry made a note to seek out his former secretary Luke Lytton to learn more details of his daughter's marriage.

Even after the earl had spoken to Alice, pointing out her place was at her husband's side, she ignored his remarks, spending as much time apart from her husband as she could. However, from accounts by Luke, Alice had brought about many efficiencies throughout the numerous households of her husband. She had made changes which saved money, spending it on the welfare of the servants, tenants and the upkeep of the buildings. However, over her husband's extravagant expenses she had no control whatsoever.

Where many had revelled in the pageant that May, a number left London to make ready for yet another campaign in the north with heavy hearts, Henry de Lacy amongst their number. True, Edward's shrewd plan was having the desired effect and there were many of the newly knighted noblemen returning home to recruit yet more men for the march to crush the Scots. Henry also knew that details of events of the past week would have been sent to the disgraced king of Scotland, Robert Bruce. Whatever Edward Plantagenet's plans to bring Scotland under his rule, he had an opponent of equal determination to thwart his ambitions. What the future now held for the realm was in the hands of God and the kings of England and Scotland.

BOOK TWO

THE AGE OF PERFIDY

CHAPTER IX

Westminster Abbey
27 October 1307

Henry de Lacy knelt with head bowed, partially to hide his grief but also to pray for his dead monarch and friend. His heart was heavy and full of misgivings. Edward I would go down in history as one of England's greatest warrior kings. Powerful, courageous, fearless in battle and wise in council, Henry felt honoured to have been called friend as well as servant to such a man. The conflict in Scotland had dwindled and faltered almost immediately after his death, but what mattered now was, how would the young Edward of Caernarfon rule? He had the appearance of a Plantagenet, tall, well-set, affable, but was this enough? Far from it! He was certainly not forged from the same metal as his sire, and that was Henry's greatest fear.

Edward I had left a legacy of war, debt and poverty. It would take wisdom and good council to guide the young king through this maze of troubles. The question in Henry's mind was: would Edward II take advice? He knew that there would be difficult times ahead. Almost the first act of the young king was to recall Piers Gaveston from Gascony where his father had banished him – the friendship already a problem. Nevertheless, Piers was now endowed with the earldom of Cornwall, for there was no one to gainsay the king's wishes. Henry glanced across at the handsome figure of the Gascon. In fairness he had sought neither title nor lands, but it altered naught, for jealousies would undoubtedly accompany his change in fortunes. Henry knew this continuing relationship in itself would generate opposition, but that would be for the morrow. Today was for mourning a unique king and life-long friend.

It had been a long and eventful journey from boyhood to old age and all the stages betwixt, for Henry was conscious that he had played a significant role in the late king's life as soldier, friend and councillor. Sometimes their opinions differed, but such differences never left any lasting rancour.

Amongst those packed in the cathedral were the nobles, prelates and magnates from Europe, England, Scotland, Wales and Ireland. Everyone acknowledged the significance of Edward's passing, for he had been such an awe-inspiring character that this was surely a momentous, historical occasion. But many in the congregation were also eyeing each other to see who would rise in the new Plantagenet reign. Undoubtedly Lincoln would remain a trusted and loyal councillor. Langton had been arrested and replaced by Walter Reynolds, the king's former keeper of the wardrobe. Robert Winchelsea, the Archbishop of Canterbury, had been recalled from exile, and Anthony Bek, who was reading the eulogy, would undoubtedly feature large in the new order. As to the Earls of Pembroke, Hereford and Warwick it remained to be seen exactly what their positions would be as they were of the same generation as the young king. Ralph Monthermer was no longer titular Earl of Gloucester as his wife Joan had died in childbirth that April and Gilbert, her young son by a former marriage, now held the title.

The French ambassador, Louis Count of Evreux, half-brother to Philip IV, was pressing for the marriage between Isabella of France and Edward to take place as soon as possible. This marriage, which had been delayed mainly because of the dead king's lack of enthusiasm for the union, many now saw as inevitable. If it brought lasting peace between France and England and severed France's ties with Scotland, surely it must be looked on with favour, but negotiations were difficult and long-winded. Henry de Lacy knew Louis to be a wily and skilful negotiator; he would need to be on his mettle where the Frenchman was concerned.

Edward I was laid to rest in an unadorned tomb in complete contrast to the tombs of his ancestors, and the old Earl of Lincoln understood the choice. It was unfussy, uncluttered, stark and plain amongst the other ornate tombs, and yet it proclaimed its own values. As the melodic voices of the choristers rose in unison the ceremony came to an end. Henry rose stiffly, his knees aching, wondering if he would live to fulfil a role at the young king's side and, indeed, where this new role would lead. Of one thing he felt certain, whatever the future held, he would not die of boredom.

Within days of the sumptuous burial ceremony yet another important ceremony took place which endorsed Piers Gaveston's place in the ranks of the nobility: his marriage to Margaret de Clare, sister to the young Earl of Gloucester, one of the wealthiest and most powerful families in the realm.

Soon after Gaveston's hasty marriage, Henry de Lacy was chosen as a member of the party that would accompany the king to France for his own marriage to the French Princess Isabella. As he stood sipping his goblet of rich wine, he voiced his fears to his daughter Alice. 'This meteoric rise of Gaveston has caused somewhat of a stir and I for one believe it spells trouble.'

Alice smiled. 'And do you think such facts worry Gaveston?'

'Not one jot but it worries me – remember, I lived through the de Montford rebellion in my youth and do not wish to see this country plunged back into such times again.' He turned the goblet in his hands as he spoke and gazed into its liquid depths. 'This is the time when your husband could hold sway.'

Alice moved closer to her father. 'Sadly we both know he lacks ability in both diplomacy and perception. His pride, arrogance, and high-handed attitude endear him to few, I fear. They are not the attributes of an advisor to a king.' The two looked at each other in complete understanding.

'Alice, can you ever forgive me for your marriage?'

'Oh, papa, of course I do. You were as helpless as I in the matter although...' she paused, 'I did not know that at the time.'

Henry bent and kissed his daughter's pale cheek. 'You are more precious to me than words can ever convey.'

Alice caught and kissed his hand. 'As you are to me, papa!'

Although the two de Lacys did not share that Yuletide, Alice received a gift of an exquisite rosary of moonstones from her father, a gift she would treasure for the rest of her life. But after the festivities were over Alice was busy preparing for the arrival of England's new queen, Isabella.

As Alice stood with the reception party on the dock waiting for Isabella of France to disembark she found herself beside the magnificent figure of Piers Gaveston, Earl of Cornwall, and his young wife, Margaret de Clare. Gaveston had been made *custos regni* in the king's absence, a fact which had enraged Thomas of Lancaster.

'You are looking chilled, my lady!' Gaveston murmured. Alice shivered against the biting wind. 'The warmth of your welcome will be appreciated by the young queen.' The handsome features broke into a smile. 'Indeed, the king needs a wife to…' he hesitated, then continued, 'to fill his life!'

'Many believe the role already filled.' Alice turned and raised a questioning eyebrow as she spoke.

'Ah, the role of "brother" can never take the place of a wife.'

'Your opinion of women differs drastically from most men's, it would seem.' Alice's voice could not be heard by anyone else for she spoke softly and the words were whipped away with the wind.

'Women are delightful, ingenious and possess far more guile than we men realise.'

'Mmm, there may be a kernel of truth in that but…' She glanced across at the tall, imposing figure of her husband and resumed her sentence, 'you, sir, are in the minority in thinking thus.'

'Believe me, my dear countess, you are far stronger than either your husband or your father realise. For my part, I seek your friendship, not your enmity, and hope you will show my wife the generosity of friendship.'

'I hope I meet everyone with the same courteous equanimity. Friendship, however, has to be earned.' She looked up into his face and smiled disarmingly.

Their conversation was interrupted by a fanfare which echoed around the waiting throng before its notes too were lost against the battering winds. As the king stepped from the gangplank he ran and threw himself into the arms of his 'brother' Gaveston. Alice noted the anger which burned in Lancaster's eyes. He was jealous and when Thomas of Lancaster was jealous he was a dangerous creature. Gaveston would need to have a good squire to watch his back. As the king and Gaveston were lost in their greetings Alice took Margaret's hand and led her forward to meet the beautiful girl who was soon to be crowned England's queen.

The scene at the dock and the king's extraordinary behaviour at his reunion with Gaveston were whispered about for months. Alice was close enough to read the surprised expression in Isabella's crystal-blue eyes, but she had quickly regained her composure and went through the formalities with consummate grace and ease for one so young. Alice saw a girl endowed with outstanding loveliness but also judged her to possess strength of character to match, something she would need in the ensuing years. What would this French princess make of her husband's special relationship with the Gascon? The coming days would provide the answer, no doubt! And the answer came with the strong disapproval of the French. The question was: how much of it was at Isabella's instigation? No one really knew, for her uncles had been sent as guardians and ambassadors for the forthcoming ceremony and it was they who voiced the concerns.

CHAPTER X

The Savoy Palace
February 1308

Preparations for the coronation were in progress and the Savoy Palace buzzed with activity like some human beehive. There were seamstresses, jewellers, silversmiths, victuallers and wine merchants coming and going throughout the bitter days of winter, but Alice was far more concerned with her father's black mood. The Earl of Lincoln was rarely out of humour, and this change concerned Alice greatly. She knew the reason lay at the heart of the relationship between the king, Gaveston and Isabella. The French had expressed their disapproval at Edward's shameful reunion with the 'upstart'. Regardless of his new title, Gaveston was classed as a commoner and therefore the French party were insulted that he should take precedence over the king's wife, for Edward had scarcely spoken to Isabella at the banquets held in her honour. Alice felt certain that the outward display of composure hid the inner turmoil the girl must have felt. Although her own wedding had been many years before, she still remembered emotions of dread and foreboding which still haunted her at times.

One morning, a few days later, Alice and her father were in the solar when he spoke of his fears. 'The king is totally unaware of how difficult these negotiations have been and if he is not more circumspect there will be repercussions that could spell disaster for England.'

'I'm sure matters will not come to that...'

Before Alice could continue, her father slapped his thigh with such resounding gusto it made one of the hounds leap to its feet and growl. 'Now see what you have done, papa, Juno thinks you are about to punish him!'

'It's not the hound I wish to punish, but the thoughtless young man we now call king.'

Alice looked round with an expression of alarm etched across her face. 'Have a care, papa, you do not wish your private views to be overheard; they could be deemed treasonous.'

Henry de Lacy studied his daughter thoughtfully. 'Egad! To think within months of his father's death Edward's behaviour has already caused a rift between himself and his nobles and upset the French.'

Alice picked up a sweetmeat from the tray and tossed it to the hound. Then she said thoughtfully, 'Thomas appears to be siding with his cousin. However, I believe this current show of unison will split wide open if he does not receive all the rewards he believes he is entitled to, and from what we have seen so far methinks his expectations will prove groundless, and when Gaveston is showered with ever more honours and lands, which he undoubtedly will, then Lancaster's true nature will be revealed.'

Henry nodded; his daughter understood the situation all too well. He looked across and stroked his beard as he spoke. 'And where does that leave you in all of this? Your duty is to your husband.'

'Pah! I feel neither duty nor loyalty to Lancaster, nor have I ever done.' She raised her left hand and displayed the bright gold ring to the light. 'I know by all the laws of man and Church I am bound to him, but how much faithfulness and loyalty has he ever displayed towards me? And why are women castigated for being honest?' She tossed her head as she walked towards him and caught his hand.

As Henry held his daughter's hand, he said, 'We will weather this storm, like all of life's storms, together for we are de Lacys, are we not?'

That evening as Matty brushed Alice's thick, waving tresses she gazed towards the great reflector but saw nothing of the fragile image it mirrored. Alice had lived with unrest and uncertainty all her life, even before her marriage. There had been the wars in Wales and Europe throughout her childhood, followed by the bitter conflict in Scotland, but they had occurred during the reign of a strong and powerful king. Now what would this new reign mean for her and her family?

Her father had sworn to uphold the rights of the king, and she knew he would not allow Edward to walk mindlessly into dangers that concerned the country. As for Thomas of Lancaster, his arrogance from the outset of their relationship had proved an overwhelming stumbling block. Nothing he did or said made him any more appealing either as a man or a husband, or in fact as a councillor to a king. She also pondered on the fate of the French princess who was faced with a situation she could never have envisaged. Men! Their thoughtless pride overshadowed the lives of women whether high- or low-born. Alice had learned to sidestep direct confrontation by using her wits and she offered up a prayer that Isabella of France would quickly learn how to veil her true emotions and find a way of dealing with her husband's unseemly behaviour. The English court, ever a hotbed of intrigue, was about to brim over with jealousies and personal ambitions and once more plunge the nation into turmoil.

'Your thoughts are flying afar, methinks!' said Matty softly.

'Mmm! Isabella is very young to be faced with the extraordinary friendship between Gaveston and her husband. I pray that with the coronation the queen will find a way of weaning Edward…' she paused, choosing her words carefully, 'from that relationship.' Then she smiled, returning once more to the present. 'And whilst we speak of relationships, pray tell me what is this I hear about you and Master Lytton?'

Matty blushed but smiled happily. 'Oh, Luke is as kind and gentle a man as you could wish to meet!'

Alice looked at her lady-in-waiting expectantly. 'And…?' she said smiling.

'W-e-l-l, when he has received permission from the earl we hope to marry in the spring!'

Alice looked at Matty's shining face. 'And no one deserves happiness more than you do, my dearest Matty!'

Alice rose and hugged her beloved servant.

With tears in her eyes Matty replied, ''Tis my greatest wish that you also should know true happiness, my lady.'

As Alice released her hold she said wistfully, 'I have long resigned myself to this life, so be happy for us both! Let us not dwell on gloomy matters for now we have two ceremonies to choose garments for!'

CHAPTER XI

Westminster Abbey
1308

As the last days of February approached Robert de Clifford scarcely slept. It was his responsibility to see that Westminster Abbey was ready for the ceremony. With a depleted treasury there had been no funds to repair the damaged abbey after the devastating fire at the end of the previous century which had left parts of the building badly scorched and ruined. Now, on a tight budget, he had organised a small army of workers to patch, paint and mend what they could in so short a time. The responsibility lay heavily as there was much dissent amongst the workmen who were being paid but a pittance for their labours. He could hear the grumbles as he passed below the scaffolds, but he merely scowled, silencing the chatter for a few moments.

The foreman came forward tentatively. 'It will never be finished, Sir Clifford.'

Robert de Clifford's face creased into a deep frown. 'Believe me, Master Pitchford, it will and *must* be finished, do you understand? Work through the night if needs be!'

The dusty figure hesitated before the imperious nobleman. 'They'll not do it for the same wages, your lordship.'

'Sack those that won't work and get those that will and trouble me no further with such trivia.' He waved his hand as he walked away from the troubled foreman.

There was nothing more to be said. Now the foreman had to relay the news that efforts needed to be redoubled and extra night-work would be paid at the same rate as during the day, something he knew would cause further grumbles. He felt like the jester on a child's toy which ran back and forth on a coloured rope.

However, with redoubled efforts progress did move forward and many of the scars of the fire were disguised in readiness for the great pageant. Ornate drapes, banners and tapestries were used to hide parts of the damage as de Clifford drew on his resourcefulness to obtain many of the items. From a distance it looked quite splendid and he hoped that no one inspected some areas too closely or they would have seen the clever disguise.

Alice looked at the deep-green kirtle of expensive velvet and mantle of gold lined with fox fur. Her headdress was of gold with emeralds, pearls and topaz, her barbette was of finest linen. The de Lacy knot motif had been embroidered all around the hem of the mantle in the same dark green.

'You will look truly magnificent!' Matty said as she clapped her hands in delight.

'But I shall feel like a mummer at a masque,' Alice said ruefully.

As the great day drew ever closer the complaints from the French contingency grew ever louder and Henry de Lacy knew that the matter of Gaveston had to be resolved or the coronation might not take place at all! As anticipated Edward refused point blank to send Gaveston from court, but even the Plantagenet fury did not deter the French from their purpose and a compromise was finally achieved. Gaveston would be sent away but after the coronation. The bitter wrangling and the intransigent manner of Edward's arguments left the ageing Earl of Lincoln feeling apprehensive that this relationship with Gaveston would prove the Achilles' heel of this reign. A split in loyalties was always a detrimental state of affairs in any situation but in the ruling of a kingdom – mortal.

To date Henry's relationship with the young Edward had been quite a comfortable one. However, the king's mood had changed and Henry now witnessed the Plantagenet anger at first hand, and what he witnessed he liked not. From the late king who had been respected, even feared, such outbursts could be forgiven, but from his untried, untested son yet to have earned the respect of his nobles and prelates it was a very different matter and one that boded ill for the future.

However, on the twenty-fifth of February 1308, the coronation of Edward II and Isabella of France took place amid all the panoply of the English court. Thomas of Lancaster carried the great sword of state Curtana, displaying all his arrogance in the royal procession. State vestments were carried by the Earl of Arundel accompanied by the young Marcher barons Roger Mortimer of Wigmore and Hugh Despencer the Younger. The Earls of Lincoln and Hereford also bore state swords and Gaveston's appearance caused quite a stir, for he wore royal purple bedecked with pearls, looking more regal than the king himself, much to the dismay of Edward's bride.

Alice walked slowly as the fanfares blared out, but inwardly hating every moment. There had been an upset when part of the scaffolding had fallen, killing an unfortunate knight, and the Bishop of Winchester had continued the service in some haste, or so it appeared to Alice. After the royal oath was sworn the rest of the ceremony continued without mishap. However, Gaveston had earned himself more dangerous enemies that day and some would prove to be his downfall.

The feasting and merriment that followed the formal occasion was a great success. Musicians from all parts of Europe and England entertained the royal party and Richard the Rhymer, the king's own favourite musician, surpassed his former performances, much to his royal master's pleasure. But for one newly crowned queen the evening proved somewhat onerous as she had to watch, neglected by her husband, as he cavorted and chatted intently to Gaveston. Alice noted how Isabella would bite her bottom lip from time to time and wondered if she were biting back a rebuke. However, Isabella was not entirely overlooked; in fact she was courted by many of the prelates and magnates who wished to become better acquainted with their new queen. Although she was naught but a child, childhood quickly passed and, as Queen of England, Isabella would have an important role to play, a fact not missed by many who attended that evening's festivities.

All that was on the mind of the Countess of Lancaster, however, was escape. Escape from ceremonial duties. Escape from duties as hostess, for with the absence of her mother from a persisting ague it had fallen to Alice to act for both her husband and father. Now she longed to leave the English capital, for she found no pleasure in its heaving streets and markets with their rank smells permeating the air. As soon as it was humanly possible Alice made ready to return to Lincolnshire, for she wished to visit her mother on her way to the north.

At Bolingbroke she found a pale, lethargic Margaret Longespee bereft of energy and thinner than Alice could ever remember. However, Margaret made little of her own indisposition and questioned Alice about the events surrounding the coronation. But although Alice was concerned for her mother's wellbeing she longed for the fresh winds of the moors and the open heath-lands she so loved. Within days she had once more made ready to continue her journey, and with a respectful farewell Alice and her party rode briskly to their destination.

It pleased Matty Holden to hear her mistress sing softly to herself as she rode northwards and she chatted merrily to those that journeyed with her. She was always mindful of the wellbeing of the sumpter horses, for they carried the burdens and trappings of the household, and she chastised anyone who abused or misused them. Although Alice never felt Pontefract was her home she did feel a sense of relief when the proud grey walls came into view. At least here she felt more in control of affairs. However, when she arrived she discovered all was not well amongst her servants.

It appeared that Walter Bourne, the head steward, had been attacked and badly injured some weeks prior to the earl's departure. One of Thomas's henchmen, Robert Holland, had recommended Ilbert Swire as his replacement, and the aforementioned had managed, within days of his appointment, to disrupt and upset virtually everyone at the castle. On hearing of this Alice was infuriated, partly because Thomas had failed to mention the attack or the new appointment, but mainly because she had engaged the quiet steward Walter, who had proved a most efficient and conscientious servant whose courteous manner had gained the respect of Alice as well as the rest of the servants and house carls. Now all she was hearing were complaints and grievances for Ilbert Swire had either dismissed many of the long-serving servants and then had them thrown out of their homes or neglected to pay them. Not only was that a disturbing turn of events, but when Alice learned that many of the merchants and traders who supplied the castle's kitchens had also not been paid either, her anger burned without disguise.

It was Matty who whispered to her mistress to hold fast and consider long and hard before making any direct moves against the offending steward. 'He has the ear of the earl and Holland and you do not want to earn their wrath.'

Alice nodded. It was true, and as she so often did when in a quandary she called for Luke, her secretary, for she knew her father had appointed him to her service to help her in times of trouble such as she now found herself in.

'What's to be done about this...this disruptive dolt?' she hissed as she fiddled with the rings on the fingers on her left hand.

Matty watched the nervous habit, knowing the rings represented fetters to Alice, ones she wished to be free of. 'My advice, my lady, is to listen carefully to all the complaints. Amid the details no doubt there will be an incident by which Swire will have condemned himself in some way.'

Luke's words halted Alice's pacing. She looked hard at the tall figure of Luke Lytton. She smiled slowly, anger replaced by satisfaction. 'Then let us not waste a moment for the sooner this... cuckoo is removed, the happier I and everyone else will feel.'

It was Matty who voiced a question which could hold the answer. 'Does anyone know exactly where this Ilbert person came from?'

Both Luke and Alice ceased reading through the piled-up ledgers. 'Oh, Matty, you possess the most common sense among us. If he had been so efficient in his previous post, how did he come here at such short notice?'

Matty and Luke looked at each other, the same idea arriving at the identical moment.

'But what if Master Bourne was attacked on orders from Holland, just so that Swire could be swiftly engaged before your return?' Luke's statement hung in the air. 'It sounds more than likely. Holland would then be acquainted with every aspect of the household and its finances and use it for whatever ends he saw fit!'

Alice clapped her hands, then said brightly, 'Let us undo all the meddling plans of Lord Holland, for I refuse to stand by and see all my efforts go for naught.'

Within days Swire's history had been discovered, and when the offending steward was summoned, he was confronted by a serious-faced countess and her close-knit staff and his former self-assurance began visibly to wilt.

'Ah, Master Swire, let me see, you were engaged by my husband last autumn, is that not correct?'

The rotund figure stood looking singularly uncomfortable and changed his weight from foot to foot as he fidgeted.

'Master Bourne, my steward, had been attacked, is that not so?'

'It is, your ladyship.'

'Most fortuitous that you were available at such short notice, is it not?' Beads of sweat began to run down the folds of flesh at his neck and on his forehead. 'Exactly where was your previous household and what position did you hold there?' Swire remained silent. 'I am waiting, Master Swire.'

Alice's voice was cool and clipped as she surveyed the figure standing before her great carved desk. Her pale-grey eyes were as hard as flint, for she was now in possession of the man's full history and it made for interesting reading.

'Were you not in the employ of one Sir Percival Pountney?'

Swire's face paled visibly as she announced the name. 'I was, but whatever lies you have been told...'

Alice raised an eyebrow as she continued, 'Lies, Master Swire? Not according to the sheriff of Stafford. Were you not dismissed for stealing jewels and silverware from Sir Percival and were you only saved from hanging by Lord Holland, for whom you had once done a service, thereby avoiding the sentence that had been issued by the court at Stafford?'

Swire's head dropped to his chest.

'I believe you were then taken into service by Lord Holland. A question whose answer I wish to know – pray, how do you serve two masters, Master Swire?'

The room remained silent. Alice desperately wanted to enquire if it had been Lord Holland who had issued the orders for the attack on Walter Bourne, but she knew better than to bring any unsubstantiated charges against a close associate of her husband's.

'I could have you whipped and charged with a number of offences, Master Swire. However, I will not do so on this occasion provided you will sign a document swearing that you will never show your face in any of the lands owned by any member of my family... Is that perfectly clear?'

Swire nodded. His head was bowed, for he knew his fate was sealed, but not by the Countess of Lancaster, who little realised she did not have to raise a hand against him, but by Lord Holland, who would dispose of him for failing in his mission; his only chance now was to disappear as soon as he left this chamber.

As the discredited scoundrel stumbled out, Alice looked at Luke. 'Do we know exactly where Walter is, Luke?'

'I believe Master Ralph took him in and his assistant is nursing him.'

Alice smiled. 'I bless that dear man every day. Now he will be doubly blest by me for those that serve me faithfully shall never find me wanting in my appreciation.'

Alice visited her injured steward and told him of the previous day's events. She also thanked the old physician and his faithful assistant Simon for their skilful nursing. 'Will Master Bourne make a full recovery?'

Ralph smiled thinly and nodded his head. 'Not completely, I fear, but enough to continue as your steward.'

'Oh, Master Ralph, that sounds somewhat pessimistic. Does that mean he may suffer from his injuries for the rest of his life?'

'Forgive an old man's scepticism, my dear countess.'

Alice reached across and took his gnarled, wrinkled hand. 'You above all men have my deepest gratitude always.' The last words were scarce more than a whisper, but Ralph's hearing was as keen as ever and he bowed and kissed her hand.

'Lady, I may have to leave these parts for I have learned that the French king has destroyed the Order of the Knights Templar. I left their order some time ago after the fall of Palestine, but surviving members are now being pursued. I do not wish to bring trouble to your household.'

Alice looked into the old man's rheumy eyes and smiled. 'No one shall ever know of your secret from me. I will send you and Simon monks' robes. Should you fear for your life go to the monastery where the monks will hide you both from danger. However, I do not foresee anyone having the temerity to detain someone in my service.'

The old man noted the steeliness in the young woman's voice and doubted not her words.

But Alice had other troubles to overcome as the news of her mother's death arrived within days of Swire's swift exit. 'May God rest her soul,' were the only words she spoke, but Matty knew Alice grieved for her mother even though their relationship had not been a close and affectionate, but one of loyalty which had grown as Alice reached maturity. So once again Alice and her retinue made ready to return to Bolingbroke for yet another funeral.

However, with Margaret Longespee's detailed arrangements for her own funeral, the ceremony was a very quiet but dignified occasion. Margaret had written, as so many of her contemporaries had already passed into the next world, she did not wish to impose false sentiments on their successors. Neither did she wish her husband and daughter to be locked into months of mourning and days of expensive ceremonies which served little or no purpose.

'The late Countess of Salisbury and Lincoln was succinct to the very end,' Matty whispered to Luke, as they watched their mistress walk behind the plain coffin. 'She was certainly no hypocrite for certain.'

Henry de Lacy and his daughter sat in the solar which had been Margaret's favourite room. The decorations were rich but not ostentatious and the colours somewhat subdued. The furniture was all of oak and only her chair was heavily carved. Silver candlesticks and heavily embroidered cushions softened the chairs and window seats. The fire glowed in the great hearth and a faint smell of pears permeated the room, for Margaret had ordered only pear logs to be burned during the last few days of her life.

'So now the title of Countess of Salisbury comes to you, Alice.'

'Titles mean so little in real terms, I fear, for most of her wealth goes to Lancaster's coffers.' Henry noted the irony in his daughter's words. 'Do not fret, papa, he cannot claim Canford and some other manors in Dorset which were not part of my dowry.'

'There is also a place I know you are fond of, Clitheroe Castle. I have already made it over to you as they did not feature in estates of the Lincoln earldom either!'

Alice smiled wanly. 'Do not worry about me, papa, I shall neither starve nor want for a roof over my head, unlike so many of the population.

'The monks at the priory will say daily prayers for the soul of my mother; she has made a generous donation to ensure their diligence.'

Father and daughter sat in silence for a while, then Henry said, 'No doubt you are aware there is a rift between many of the nobles and the king because of his insistence on bestowing so many honours, titles and lands on the Gascon.' He paused before continuing. 'I have cause to believe they have the right of the matter, therefore I find myself in an uncomfortable position in opposition to the king, something I never thought possible. The French have insisted the Gascon must leave court, and I know Edward will need a great deal of persuading to agree to their demands. Even if he complies with their demands, I fear he will not let the matter rest. Somehow he will find a way of bringing him back.'

Alice looked hard at her father. 'And do you believe that Gaveston wanted all of these titles and wealth?'

'No, I do not judge him to be avaricious, nor has he ever intimated that he desired the title of earl. However, as we know, when a Plantagenet's mind is set nothing will dissuade him from his purpose.'

'Can he not see the dangerous position in which he places his friend?'

'The king possesses none of his father's perception of human nature or even the character of those that surround him. In fact he appears to be drawn to opposite ranks and is far more at ease with his carpenters, grooms, pantlers and brushwood sweepers.'

'Which leaves you where exactly?'

Henry shrugged his great bear-like shoulders. 'For once in my life I cannot answer you with any certainty. I have summoned all those who are dissatisfied with this unsatisfactory state of the realm since the king came to power, and we are to meet at Pontefract for discussions on our next move. Therefore I must leave immediately. May I call on you once more to play my hostess? I know your husband sides with his cousin.'

'He will be angered by such a move.' She smiled. 'Therefore, I will be delighted to do so!'

'The late king's widow, Margaret of France, has sent a great deal of silver to fund us which also puts her in the position of choosing her late husband's wishes over her stepson's. I believe she has done so to avoid civil war and also war with France.'

'Poor England! Beleaguered, in debt and on a course even the royal helmsman has no notion of, or even which way the wind of opinion blows!' Alice spoke the words with genuine sadness in her voice.

Matters moved rapidly over the coming months, but eventually Edward grudgingly agreed to send Gaveston into exile, easing the tension between the king and his nobles and averting Henry de Lacy's greatest fear – civil war.

In June the king summoned his armies to muster once more at Carlisle to face the Scots who had been regaining many of the castles and lands previously held by the English. At Northampton the king became reconciled with the leading earls who had voiced their dissatisfactions over Gaveston's earldom – Gloucester, Hereford, Richmond, Warwick and Lincoln.

During the autumn the king tried to placate his nobles and for the most part succeeded, all that is except for the proud Lancaster who had taken personal affront at something the king had either said or done. No one in fact was certain why but Lancaster now took a stance against his cousin the king. For Henry de Lacy it could have posed a prickly, personal dilemma causing him much discomfort. He sent a messenger to his daughter warning her of the current situation. Meantime his fears for the future grew.

Lancaster was even more infuriated when Gaveston returned from his enforced exile during which, much to the king's amusement, his companion had made a great success of his lieutenancy of Ireland. This merely served to stoke the fires of enmity between the Plantagenet cousins.

The Scottish wars rumbled on without any real success for the English. Whenever it looked as though there might be a pitched battle the Scots melted away, only to attack some less well-defended castle miles away.

'I tell you it's like fighting the will o' the wisp!' exclaimed John de Warenne.

'Aye!' muttered the Earl of Richmond. 'They tease us like children, then run away and destroy our toys leagues away.'

The crooked smile on the young Earl of Surrey's dark features marked his agreement. He wheeled his magnificent destrier as he spoke. 'Come, methinks we waste our time and efforts here, but give the sentries and outriders orders to be extra-vigilant. Caution must be our watchword, for the enemy may double back and attack us as we sleep.'

'Lincoln is not happy with the situation and I for one trust that old warrior's instincts. The king has misjudged our position yet again.'

'Aye, Longshanks must be clawing his way out of his grave seeing all his former successes waning like a winter moon.' The two earls rode side by side back to their tents in silence, both lost in their own thoughts.

But the old Earl of Lincoln had other matters on his mind at that time: marriage! Henry de Lacy had quietly married the young daughter of a baron from the west country, one Joan Martin.

When Alice learned of this event she was shocked to her core. 'Pray tell me, is he losing his reason in his dotage?' She walked around her chamber, wringing her hands as she did so.

'Maybe, like the late king he thought to father a son…' Matty's words trailed off as she saw the look of incredulity spread across Alice's pale features.

Alice finally stopped her pacing. 'Men never cease to amaze me! First Thomas is supporting his cousin wholeheartedly, then, at some perceived slight, poof! He changes his tune like some fiddler. Now my own father appears to have lost his wits and marries a girl young enough to be his daughter.'

Nonetheless, by the time that Henry rode into the courtyard with his young bride Alice had regained her composure. As she looked down from her window she turned to Matty and whispered, 'Heavens! She looks younger than me!'

But she received the new Countess of Lincoln with a warm welcome. After all she was now her stepmother!

CHAPTER XII

Scotland
1311

'It is so cold in this God-forsaken country I swear I will never get warm again!' The complaint came from Fulke de Pembrugge.

Eubolo LeStrange looked across at the speaker. He was thankful that his stay in Scotland was to be but a short one for his lord, the Earl of Lancaster, who had refused to come in person, had sent but the obligatory number of troops, and he was one of their number. Eubolo, together with a dozen or so squires who were also learning the craft of knighthood, had come for the experience.

'The right clothing would help, Pembrugge! Your jerkin and breeches are of the poorest quality.'

'I prefer spending my silver on the more enjoyable pleasures of life,' Fulke de Pembrugge muttered with a toothy grin.

'Then suffer the consequences, for cold kills far more than do your enemies' weapons.'

'He speaks the truth!' The weathered face of the company's sergeant peered out of the gloom. 'Now go see to the horses and mind you keep your eyes peeled, fer them Scottish varmints be like quicksilver and will slit thee from stem to stern with a single stroke!'

Adam Walkefare had been a soldier all his life. Even as a lad, he had tottered around the barracks; he knew no other life nor did he want one. He walked back to his own tent where his second-in-command sat warming his gnarled fingers before a glowing brazier.

'The contingent sent by the Earl of Lancaster is a mixed bunch and no mistake! Some little more than boys.' He spoke more to himself than his corporal. For the most part these 'boys' lacked both the heart and the mind of true warriors, but it was his job to lick 'em into shape. Nonetheless, amongst their numbers were a few that had the makings of decent fighters. He expected nothing less from those from the Welsh Marches. They were weaned on fighting and would have quickly learned the art of guerrilla warfare similar to the Scotsmen's tactics.

His corporal spoke, his voice low and gruff. 'We lost more horses today and about a dozen men are unaccounted for – the weak-kneed bastards!' He spat into the brazier.

'Well, Rufus, they ain't veterans like you an' me and can you really blame the buggers? They are close to starvation with no real leader to whip their blood fer a battle.'

'Battle! That would at least relieve this bloody boredom.'

'Still thy tongue, you old bastard, we shall see action, mark my words. Maybe not today or tomorrow, but this Bruce has a bunch of hardened fighters and fer my money they will give a good account of themselves, but not at our English master's pleasure. He'll choose the time and the place, then look to all your soldiering skills, fer ye will need 'em, believe me!'

'Well, if you think I'm afeared of they Scotsmen think again, Sergeant Walkefare, 'cause Rufus Staveley ain't frightened of any man.'

The sergeant grinned and slapped his corporal on the shoulder. If he had an army of Rufus Staveleys he'd pit himself against any foe, for the doughty corporal was as skilled a fighter as he.

'Stop yer noise and give thought to where we find tomorrow's meal for both men and 'osses.'

As the bitter winter in Scotland dragged on it saw more and more men slip silently away from their positions, leaving the English contingent both vulnerable and exposed. However, the English king was about to be dealt an even greater blow. The news that struck the young king left him grieving on a personal level and alarmed for the governance of his realm. Henry de Lacy, Earl of Lincoln, had died, a man whom he had known all his life. Their relationship had until recently been a close, amicable one. He was amongst the last of his father's friends and councillors who was equally adept as a knight and as an ambassador. Edward knew that had de Lacy not intervened recently with his nobles and magnates, he could have been faced with civil war. Who now would step into this unique role? Who had earned the respect of Church and nobility in England and on the Continent? Who would wear the mantle of trusted aide and confidant? Piers was reviled by the French and English alike and de Lacy had proved an effective buffer between them over the years. Even in the latter weeks when he had opposed him in matters of the Ordinances there had never been any animosity, just genuine concern for the true governance of the kingdom. Edward mourned the man who had given years of unstinting loyalty and service to both his father and himself. But if Edward was alarmed by Henry's death, his daughter Alice was bereft. She did not weep or moan, she just went into deep shock and lived through the hours and days which followed the news like a hollow husk.

Arrangements were made for the funeral, but to Alice everything and everyone seemed like puppets at a macabre masque. The grand funeral took place, but Alice walked through the ceremony like a wraith, silent, pale, dark-eyed. She stood beside her stepmother Joan Martin, but there was a marked difference between the grieving women. The daughter was undoubtedly heartbroken whereas the young wife, who had hardly had time to adapt to her new role as Countess of Lincoln, looked hardly moved.

It was months later that Alice experienced flashes of that day. She remembered the quiet commiserations of Queen Isabella, of Henry of Lancaster, her brother-in-law, who had held her hand and murmured his condolences. Then she remembered the words of John de Warenne, Earl of Surrey. 'Your father was a great man who spoke his mind with fearless honesty, something which now will be greatly missed. Lady, should you ever need my aid, know I am always at your service.' He had bent and kissed her hand before moving away, but she remembered the earnest look in his dark-blue eyes as he spoke. The king had also spoken of a mutual loss, but it took Alice long months before she was ready to face the future without the invisible shield her father had placed around her. Theirs had been a deep, affectionate, easy relationship, where even many months spent apart had never weakened the bond of love between them.

CHAPTER XIII

Scotland
August 1311

Robert the Bruce stood before the grim-faced group of men he commanded, James Douglas, Thomas Randolph and Gilbert Hay. He inspected their ragged troops, men who had answered the call to arms in the name of Scottish freedom, men Bruce knew and trusted, men who had proved their worth in battles against the English, their hated enemy.

'Gentlemen, whilst Edward argues with his earls and magnates we will seize this opportunity to strike and strike hard where they least expect it. Target vulnerable positions across the border and hit in quick succession.' There was a rumble of assent as he continued, 'The key is surprise – we must choose our targets with care and strike all across the northern counties so that the English know not where they will be attacked next. Each commander will need accurate information, so spies and communications are vital to our plans. Fast riders cannot always reach their destinations, so I suggest in most instances reflectors.' The Bruce studied the reactions of his commanders, his keen gaze missing nothing. He noted both surprise and scepticism, but James Douglas only grinned.

'Aye, they'll be far too busy to watch for wee flashes.'

'Are you agreed, gentlemen?' The features of the Bruce, tanned by months in the saddle and living rough, showed how he had been honed into a hardened guerrilla warrior who had led many of the daring raids during the past few years. Robert the Bruce asked no man to do anything he would not himself do or had not already done, and his commanders both loved and respected him for it.

'We will strike fear and awe into our enemy and leave them believing that we have supernatural powers to aid us.'

'You mean like the *devil's army?*'

Thomas Randolph nodded his head slowly. 'Put a man in fear and he will defeat himself, methinks!'

'Aye, now you begin to get the measure of my thinking. Speed, fear and confusion will be our watchword. They will serve us better than the unwilling troops at Edward's command. Now let us draw up plans for which we will need good intelligence of every target. James, make ready to send your fastest riders to each of the chosen destinations for we must be certain that we are not riding into English traps.' He strode across to the brazier to warm his icy hands, for the spring nights were still chilly.

By August the raids which had started were proving successful. The English were caught out by both the speed and ferocity with which they were being attacked. So began the chain of events Bruce had so carefully planned. Whispers also began to spread along the Borders that no earthly men could travel so swiftly and strike in so many places simultaneously, and with each raid the rumours multiplied. The news of Bruce's excommunication added to the tales, so folk spoke fearfully, believing he must surely be in league with the Devil, and the notion had grown as the Scottish king had hoped it would.

The news of these audacious attacks by the Scots added further annoyance to the king's mounting problems, but he was virtually helpless to act. The earls and magnates, now in vehement opposition to his rule, were insisting that Gaveston should once again be sent into exile. This extra demand, added to the list of Ordinances previously requested, were worded in such plain terms it is was obvious Edward was left with no alternative but to comply or he could expect no co-operation from the complainants. It was not surprising that amongst the most vociferous of their number were the Earls of Warwick, Hereford and Lancaster. Given this united stance, Edward had to forego any plans to counteract the Scottish raids, which now appeared of little importance. The king had obviously failed to ignite any patriotic fervour amongst his nobles.

Whilst the Earl of Lancaster and his fellow Ordainers were in urgent talks with the king, his countess emerged from months of mourning and began to take more notice of her surroundings. Kenilworth had always been a place she had felt comfortable in and its views across the vast lake from her bower always brought so much pleasure. The warm sandstone pillars gave the imposing castle a more welcoming aspect.

One of the first things she noted was that Brother Benedict had been replaced by a much younger monk who had a far more imposing persona than his ageing predecessor.

'Pray when did Brother Benedict leave?' Alice looked enquiringly at Matty.

'Almost a month ago, my lady!'

'Have I been so lost in my own grief?'

'You have scarcely spoken these past months. We almost despaired that you would ever return to us.'

'And who has taken Brother Benedict's place?'

'Brother Vincent.'

'And what is known of Brother Vincent, pray?'

Matty put down her needlework as she replied, 'Well, he is firm, plain-speaking and I get the feeling he fears no one.'

Alice looked across at her lady-in-waiting. 'Then have him sent for immediately and we will learn his history.'

Matty went to the door to instruct the page to fetch Brother Vincent. As she returned she said softly, 'It is good to know you have returned to us, my lady.'

Alice smiled wistfully. 'Back to a world without my father's shield of protection, back to a world of dangerous intrigue, I fear.'

Matty looked at the pale features. 'Why so afeared, my lady?'

'Why? Because Lancaster has no one to gainsay his wishes or temper his rash actions. Consider, two Plantagenets in opposition with all the traits of that family. Don't tell me there will be no serious conflict. My father's advice and moderating voice are now silenced forever with no successor to his role of mediator. Gaveston is the main linchpin in this division and my father foresaw the problems his relationship with the king would cause and the jealousies it would provoke.' Alice hesitated. This had been the most she had spoken in months.

'Do you think Gaveston is aware of his dangerous position?' Matty said as she picked up her needlework again. 'Surely the king will protect his friend?'

Alice shook her head slowly as she replied. 'No one realises to what lengths Lancaster will go or who he will infect with his enmity and the knowledge causes me to fear the future greatly.' Before Matty could make any further comment a knock at the door silenced their discourse.

Brother Vincent entered, his rosary beads clicking as he walked briskly to stand before the countess.

'Ah, Brother Vincent, I have been somewhat preoccupied, hence your arrival has gone almost unnoticed. Pray, how is Brother Benedict?'

The young monk looked at the woman seated before him. 'He has been assigned to lighter duties as he found traversing the countryside with your household a growing strain on his health. Consequently the abbot thought a younger man could serve your ladyship more ably.'

Alice studied the speaker intently. Brother Vincent was tall and slender, but there was no frailty about him either in physique or in his features. He had a steady gaze and his dark eyes did not waver under scrutiny.

'You will no doubt find this household somewhat perplexing, but I will leave you to discover that for yourself.' She studied his expression as she spoke, for Alice de Lacy greeted any newcomer into her service with more than a modicum of suspicion. 'Brother Benedict had my complete trust; you, Brother Vincent, you will have to earn it.'

Matty looked across at her mistress with undisguised surprise. This clipped speech was so unlike Alice's normal behaviour. However, the monk did not appear ruffled and bowed slightly. 'Then I pray you will not find me lacking in loyalty, my lady. My prayers will be offered for your wellbeing.'

'I shall hear Mass at seven of the clock during winter months and six during spring, summer and autumn. Now tell me, who exactly is Brother Vincent?'

The question did not faze the young cleric. 'I am the youngest of five brothers and therefore was destined to become a servant of God.'

Alice looked at him intently. 'I have a feeling that a sword would have been your chosen weapon, not a string of rosary beads.'

'My destiny is in God's hands, as are we all!'

'Indeed, you are from a noble family?'

'My father is a baron, but not a wealthy one.' He grinned disarmingly as he spoke.

'From which area of the realm do you hail from?'

'The Welsh Marches, my lady.'

'Ah, a warrior family no less!'

'Yes, indeed my father is in the service of the De Grey family.'

'Well, Brother Vincent, you will no doubt find your own battlefield in my service.' He noted the irony in her tone, and without any further ado she dismissed him with a wave of her hand. He made the sign of the cross in a blessing before his black-robed figure left the chamber.

Matty said, 'Were you not somewhat brusque, my lady?'

Alice looked at her lady-in-waiting. 'Life is harsh, Matty, and serving a de Lacy will be doubly so now! Brother Vincent has been given the opportunity to choose his allegiance. I did not wish to cozen him by sweet words.'

Matty nodded. It was true the order of change had already begun whilst Alice had been in a state of personal mourning. But matters were about to become significantly worse in a way which would affect both high- and low-born, and especially those that served the imperious Earl of Lancaster.

CHAPTER XIV

Bolingbroke
June 1312

Alice de Lacy stood in the herb garden and took in a deep breath. 'The smell of summer,' she murmured. Matty was busy gathering baskets of thyme, rosemary, mint and sage. The two women were lost in their own reveries when a commotion in the courtyard attracted their attention. Matty put down her basket of herbs and was running to see what the noise was all about when a dishevelled figure thrust past her and dropped to his knee before Alice.

'Pray what is all this haste and…' She stopped as she recognised the face of her own messenger, Kit Cavendish. 'Kit… Whatever is amiss?'

'Oh, my lady, such calamitous news I fear.'

'Well, end my curiosity, pray.'

''Tis the Earl of Cornwall…'

'Gaveston!' she exclaimed.

'He's been captured and executed.'

Alice went pale but remained composed. 'Details, Kit, I prithee.'

'As you know the earl had returned from his exile and rejoined the king, but also to be with his wife for the birth of their first child. His whereabouts were discovered by the Lord Ordainers who surrounded him, and after a brief battle he was taken. The Earls of Pembroke and Surrey were his escorts, but Surrey departed and left Gaveston with the Earl of Pembroke. When they reached Deddington Castle, Pembroke learned his wife was travelling nearby and went to visit her, leaving but a few men to guard his prisoner. During the night the Earl of Warwick's men overwhelmed the guards and seized Gaveston, who was then taken before the Earls of Lancaster and Warwick. They accused him of his transgressions.'

At these words a soft groan escaped Alice's lips, but she remained silent. 'After what was described as a trial, Gaveston was taken to a place known as Blacklow Hill and executed.' He hesitated. 'The Earl of Lancaster refused to believe Gaveston was dead until he had seen his head.'

Both Alice and Matty crossed themselves at these words.

'There is worse to come, I fear. The body was left for some time until a band of shoemakers gathered it up and carried it to Warwick Castle where the earl refused to accept it and ordered them to return it the place they had found it!' Alice gasped. 'However, one of the shoe smiths went to the Dominican monastery close by and told them what had transpired and the monks went and claimed Gaveston's body and stitched back his head and cleansed his remains.'

'A most charitable act considering that the dead earl had been excommunicated on his return to England,' Alice murmured. More loudly she said, 'Thank you, Kit, for your services. However, I fear this devastating news will have far-reaching consequences. By this heinous act Lancaster has cast a shameful shadow not only over his own name but mine also. The king will undoubtedly seek revenge for Gaveston's unlawful execution, be assured of that.' She turned to her lady-in-waiting who had been standing dumbstruck at the messenger's words. 'Come, Matty, first we will have Brother Vincent say prayers for the dead earl.' She turned back to Kit and spoke very softly, 'Kit, I want you to find the Countess of Cornwall and convey my deepest sympathies. I wish that poor girl to know I had no knowledge of events until this day and if there is aught I can do for her and her child I will move heaven and earth to do it.' She touched Kit on the shoulder as she continued to speak. 'Wear only the colours of de Lacy, for I fear Lancaster's will be reviled by many, especially Gaveston's widow... And Kit...travel with care and God's blessings on you. I intend to return to Pontefract for I am certain Lancaster will flee from the king's wrath to that place. If the Countess of Cornwall needs you, then do her bidding, but return to me as soon as you are able, for I feel I shall be in need of your services ere long.'

The two women left the garden, for the day had lost its magic and the baskets of herbs were left for another maid to collect. Alice heard Mass and prayed fervently for Gaveston's soul and for the girl and her child who had been left victims of the pride and vanity of men. Alice kept remembering Gaveston's words on being pawns in the king's game. Well, his earthly part was over, but Alice felt deeply uneasy. She of all people knew the vagaries of the Plantagenet character; the king would never forgive those that had slain his beloved 'brother'. She felt a deep anger at Lancaster's cowardice. He could never fight fairly, and the vows taken as a knight were cast aside whenever he saw fit. Damn that arrogant man to all eternity. And how had Warwick come to be so embroiled in this treachery?

The voice of Brother Vincent filtered through her troubled thoughts, but try as she might the feelings that the news had ignited burned within her. She knew they would never be extinguished. This had been the final straw and she was now determined to break with Lancaster whatever the cost. He had betrayed her father's honour and had put his pride before the needs of his country instead of seeking ways to bring the king to an amicable acceptance of the Ordinances. Inside her anger burst like a pent-up dam. It made her determined to confront the man who had filled her life with pain and unhappiness, but she knew to openly confront him would bring down his wrath upon her head. However, to remain silent would be to deny her own conscience.

Alice learned that, instead of returning to Kenilworth, Lancaster had in fact gone to Worcester for a meeting with the Ordainers. Whilst Gaveston's body lay embalmed and draped in cloth of gold at Oxford, mourned by his monarch, two of the most powerful earls, Pembroke and Surrey, who had formerly supported Lancaster and Warwick in their complaints against the king for failing to uphold the resumption of the Ordinances, now openly condemned Gaveston's execution and returned to support the king.

At first Edward blamed Aymer de Valence, the Earl of Pembroke, and accused him of colluding with Warwick and Lancaster, but after hearing Pembroke's explanation that because he had trusted the word of Gaveston not to escape he had left but a handful of men to guard him, never believing there was any real danger. Eventually the king accepted the distraught earl's pleas of innocence.

Alice's fears for Gaveston's widow were unfounded as the king took her wellbeing to be his priority. The jewels and horses stolen when Gaveston was captured were ultimately returned as they belonged to the king, but the whole incident was to have far-reaching effects upon both the king and his fractious nobles. Alice knew the Plantagenet memory was both long and patient and the king would avenge his lost 'brother', regardless of however many treaties and vows he made. In his eyes they had broken all their oaths of honour and knighthood. Therefore what value had mere words?

Instead of making for Pontefract Alice changed her route and headed for Kenilworth, the great castle which stood in the midlands of England. But the magnificent castle on this occasion held no delights for the Countess of Lancaster. Her mission was to confront the man who in her eyes and the eyes of many had dishonoured the name of Lincoln. She knew that the earl would come to Kenilworth as it was both the grandest and the closest to Warwick and Hereford.

Within days the earl, with a heavily armed company of soldiers and squires, rode through the great gateway. Alice watched as grooms leapt forward to take Lancaster's great charger. She could tell by the way he shouted instructions to his servants he was at his belligerent best. He swept into the castle, his cloak billowing out around him. Alice made the sign of the cross, looked at Matty and said softly, 'A de Lacy, a de Lacy.' It was how knights in battle signalled to both their enemies and their own men that they were on the field of battle. Matty knew by the tension in her mistress's shoulders that Alice was preparing for an unprecedented confrontation with Lancaster and she followed the fast-walking countess to the earl's apartments. Without any preamble Alice walked straight in to stand before the imposing figure of the man who in the eyes of the world was her husband.

'What...?'

The earl got no further as Alice, eyes blazing, erupted. 'Your cowardly act of murder has brought the name of Lincoln into disrepute. My father would have burned his titles and wealth if he had for one moment believed they would be so ill-used.' Lancaster half rose but Alice's small frame quivered with anger as she continued. 'Can you not see what you have done? You think by killing Gaveston all your ills are at an end. Do you truly believe the king will now listen with a more favourable ear to your complaints? Then think again. You, the premier earl of England, now stand as the Scots' greatest asset. You who by this single act of treachery have split the loyalties of the greatest houses of the land and have left your anointed king vulnerable to his enemies, it is ill done, sir, and you of all people should know that a Plantagenet will never forgive your act of betrayal. Edward will see you dead for this, so walk with care, my lord Earl of Lancaster, and from this day forward I denounce you for the traitor you are, and if you believe that men such as Holland will protect you, think again – rats always leave when the vessel sinks.' And without further ado she turned and stalked out of the chamber, leaving Thomas of Lancaster and Robert Holland open-mouthed at her outburst.

When Alice reached her own apartments she ordered her servants to make ready to leave directly, for although the interview had cost her much and every nerve in her body trembled she was also exalted that finally she had spoken her true feelings and knew she had caught him off-guard. Her words would carry that much more weight by the very fact she was normally so reserved and undemonstrative. No doubt the castle would soon reverberate with news of her condemnation. Within the hour Alice was mounted and heading for her own castle at Canford. She wanted her abrupt departure known, to emphasise that she was no party to the earl's actions against the Crown. The de Lacy family had always been totally loyal.

Kit Cavendish learned of events at Kenilworth for such news was like summer wildfires spreading with alarming speed. Instead of heading for Pontefract he turned his horse's head south to Dorset and Canford. Inwardly he saluted the petite countess for it must have taken a great deal of courage to confront the powerful earl. 'We serve a brave lady, Mercury,' he said, patting the glossy neck of his horse.

On his arrival at Canford it was only days before the two were once more on the road, this time to seek the Earl of Surrey, John de Warenne.

Alice's letter simply read:

My Lord,
You once offered your support. I may be in need of your help as

I have denounced Lancaster's cowardly act and as we both know Plantagenets are unforgiving in their nature. Therefore I appeal to you for help should I find myself in danger.

It was simply signed Alice de Lacy, Countess of Lincoln and Salisbury.

The reply was brief and succinct.

Dearest Countess,
  My sword is at your command.
  Warenne

On receiving this assurance Alice felt easier in her mind. Of all the noblemen at court John de Warenne was the one she felt she could trust. He too was married to a Plantagenet, Joan de Bar, who like herself had not sought the marriage but had been but a pawn in the late king's plan of binding wealth, titles and power to the royal family. She knew that Warenne was seeking a divorce and that Lancaster, that hypocritical, arrogant, cowardly man, was using the Church and his influence to oppose it. What could be more of an insult than to seek help from the man with whom her husband was in open conflict!

Matty had always known that Alice possessed courage and spirit which now shone through, for she was no longer constrained by convention. Her true nature, now free, added a liveliness and vivacity which made her look younger and lovelier.

Alice rode out every day and kept abreast of events from a distance. She also kept up a busy correspondence with the stewards of all Lancaster households and continued to administer them, only visiting when sure that the earl was elsewhere. For all of Alice's own personal life she never stinted on what she saw as her duty to the people that came under her jurisdiction.

Throughout the rest of 1312 and 1313 the wrangling between the king and his magnates continued, but eventually treaties were reached and it was only then that the Scottish situation was finally addressed and the king was urged once again to field an army in an effort to defeat Robert Bruce.

CHAPTER XV

'Now at last the bastards must stand and fight.' Rufus Staveley rubbed his hands as he spoke.

'Never bank on what the Scots will do, my lad, they are as slippery as any eel I have ever come across. Besides...' Sergeant Adam Walkefare hesitated before continuing, 'from previous experience Bruce would not gamble on a full-scale battle if he was not confident he had a better than even chance of winning.'

Rufus grunted. 'Look at all the heavy cavalry.'

Before he could continue Adam interrupted. 'Exactly...heavy cavalry when the Scots use hobelars, light cavalry, which can move swiftly and easily through difficult terrain.'

Rufus looked at his sergeant with a quizzical expression. 'Surely our commanders have taken this into account.'

'I for one would not bank on it. Have you not heard their quarrels and raised voices? I like it not when commanders cannot agree where and how to proceed. Personal pride features too heavily in this campaign for my liking, and we...' he waved his hand at the company of troops scattered around the tent, 'are the poor buggers who have to put our lives into their hands. I tell you, corporal, I have a feeling in my bones, for all their fine armour and great horses and greater numbers the odds lie with the Scots. Bruce will not risk the lives of his men either from pride or on a whim; for my silver he is the wiliest of commanders.'

Rufus Staveley hunched his great shoulders at the words. 'Not often I hear doubt in your words, sergeant.'

'No doubt, only facts.' And even as he spoke the voices of the Earls of Hereford and Gloucester could be heard, with the lower tones of the Earl of Pembroke who was obviously trying to placate both men. 'See what I mean?'

Adam Walkefare said no more, but his corporal felt uneasy, then muttered, 'You have forgotten our Welsh archers. They will sting the Scottish heathens for certain.'

'Indeed if they are in the right position to be effective. If not...' his words trailed off.

'So you think...?'

'Come, corporal, there is enough talk amongst the noblemen. We are but soldiers and as soldiers must obey our commander. Let us trust in our own abilities and experience and pray to God that we give a good account of ourselves when the time comes.' Their discourse was interrupted by a herald seeking the sergeant, who on reading his orders moved out of his own tent and towards the tent of the arguing earls.

As Adam Walkefare made ready to deploy his troops, the LeStrange kinsmen sat discussing what their roles would be in the coming fight.

'This rift between the king and his cousin does us no favours.' Fulke LeStrange looked across at his younger cousin Eubolo. 'I feel somewhat ashamed that Lancaster has sent so few of us to represent him.'

Eubolo nodded. 'Surrey also has not shown but at least his contingent is larger and better equipped. Our fathers and forefathers have set our families' standard for us and therefore we fund weapons, horses and extra men from our own pockets.'

'What changes through the ages, cousin? Not loyalty and honour in service to the Crown.' Fulke grinned at his kinsman. The two could not have been more dissimilar in appearance. Fulke, heavy-framed, swarthy, with a mass of dark hair, whereas Eubolo was tall, fairer of skin and hair, with finer features. 'I believe Lancaster sent us for just such reasons. He knows we do not like being at odds with our king.'

'*We* are not at odds, merely in the service of an earl that upholds the Ordinances.'

'Well, what about the legal case?' Eubolo looked across at Fulke.

'Legal matters are one thing, right is right, and even the king should accept that we are not about to concede land wrongly allocated without pursuing our rights. Our loyalty, however, and our family's loyalty have always been with the king.'

'You mean you believe Lancaster has sent us in the hope that we may be slain?'

Fulke nodded. 'There is a good chance, for you can be certain the king will send Lancaster's contingent into the most dangerous position.'

Eubolo's eyebrows rose in surprise. 'You really believe that?'

'I do! But be certain we will look to each other's welfare and fight as closely together as possible knowing that united we can prevail. Old Master Strongarm taught us well as did our fathers, and our fighting skills will stand us in good stead. We will bring honour to the LeStrange standard.'

Eubolo raised his goblet. 'Amen to that, dear cousin.'

Meantime, as the knights and their troops assembled in readiness for the forthcoming battle, a small cavalcade rode through the mighty gateway at Pontefract. Lady Stapleton, who had accompanied her husband and stepson to the Borders, had come on a whim to visit the Countess of Lancaster.

The Stapleton family had been both friends and adherents of Alice's father, Henry de Lacy, until his death. What had prompted the visit Lady Joan could not really say, only she had an overwhelming impulse to see Alice once more. Upon their arrival Matty Holden clapped her hands and look towards the heavens. 'Forgive me, Lord, for using the old arts, for you know it was in the service of my beloved mistress.' She crossed herself but felt elated that this no-nonsense lady had arrived at such an opportune moment.

Joan Stapleton took one look at Alice and gasped. 'My dearest child, whatever has happened, you look positively ill.'

Alice, pale with visible bruises still marking her cheeks and eyes, smiled wanly at her visitor. 'A fall from a horse, I fear.'

Joan shook her head. 'Well, to me it looks more like...' Alice looked pleadingly at the older woman who stopped immediately, suddenly realising that to speak openly might put Alice in the way of more abuse. Lady Stapleton bustled forward and sat down close to Alice. 'Fear not, child, now I am here I have the very remedies to take out the bruises. I did not have a brood of stepsons and not learn that skill at an early age.'

Alice took a deep sigh. For the first time in weeks she felt safe, in fact, since her return to Pontefract which had been at the urging of Brother Vincent. Even Lancaster would not touch her whilst Joan Stapleton was visiting and something told her that that doughty woman would not leave until she was totally healed. The truth was that Joan was worried about the fate of her husband and sons and found being busy was the certain antidote for her own condition. Joan frowned as the sound of hammering echoed around the walls of the chamber Alice explained the work was a result of the earl's plans for improvements.

'Pray tell me, why are all the workmen below your windows?'

'I believe the earl thought it saved time as they did not have to convey the stones very far.'

Joan bustled around the chamber running her thumb along the furniture and drapes. 'Well, I can tell you I would make my objections known were I in such a situation.' She smiled mischievously. 'And I shall tell that to the earl this very day.' And without further ado she stalked from the room.

Matty grinned at Alice. 'That interview I would love to see.' Whatever Joan said to Thomas of Lancaster no one ever found out for certain, but by midday the workmen and the stones were being moved to another site and the next day a gardener was busy restoring the herbs and flower beds to their former state.

As the weeks moved into June, Joan persuaded Thomas to allow Alice to accompany her back home, and the two women set out together, both with feelings of relief at leaving behind the imposing walls of Pontefract. The further away they travelled the higher Alice's spirits rose. Joan, on the other hand, still feared for the safety of her husband and stepsons and even though she was plagued by her anxieties, she chatted companionably with Alice, which helped them both to varying degrees. Neither woman knew how the forthcoming events were to change their lives forever. Matty remained quiet and withdrawn throughout the journey. She had been experiencing vivid nightmares which both frightened and alarmed her, but she kept her personal forebodings to herself.

Near Stirling Castle on the twentieth-fourth of June, Matty's premonitions came to fruition. The glittering array of English chivalry moved ever closer to meet the Scottish horde. Horns blared, bright colourful banners danced and flapped in the breeze and the clank of harness and weapons filled the morning air. Sergeant Adam Walkefare and his corporal Rufus Staveley headed a company of troops under the king's colours. 'God have mercy on us,' he muttered, and Rufus looked across at his sergeant with deepening alarm. In all the years they had served together he had never seen such an expression on his sergeant's face and it puzzled him. True, the terrain most certainly did not favour heavy cavalry as the ground was wet and boggy and the river estuary ran too close to a contingent of tight-knit ranks. The sloping ground favoured the enemy and it boded ill for the English force. Then Rufus remembered words spoken by his sergeant some months past, that Robert Bruce would only fight in open battle if he felt confident that he had more than an even chance of victory. He dismissed his misgivings – surely weight of numbers would win the day? His doubts brushed away, he concentrated on the matters in hand. He touched his trusty sword in a reassuring gesture. They had served together through more campaigns than he cared to remember and lived to tell the tale. What was different about this Scottish ragtag army?

Almost the first casualty of the battle was the young nephew of the Earl of Hereford, Henry de Bohun, who had seen Bruce riding some way from his men and, without a second thought, had charged at the Scottish king. Here in this instance he, Henry de Bohun, could win this battle by slaying Bruce and winning a glorious victory. Many watched with bated breath as the seasoned warrior swung his mighty battle axe. His speedy little mount was manoeuvred so that Bruce, standing in his stirrups, was able to smash the axe down with such force it sliced through the glittering helm so deep it almost reached de Bohun's sternum. Blood spurted in a fountain, staining the once bright armour.

Bruce reined in his mount, saluted the fallen body of de Bohun, then turned and cantered back to his lines. The tenor of the day had been set. Adam Walkfare's assessment of Bruce proved right, the battle that ensued was one of the most cruel and vicious ever fought. English pride was now replaced by shame, honour by disgrace, and many noble families lost sons, fathers, brothers, uncles. It was a day filled with noise unlike any heard before. Filled with the terrifying screams of dying men and horses. The ground stained with the blood and entrails of both. The smell of death pervaded the air and tainted the nostrils of those that survived the day's horror.

The king was incensed as he watched as his heavy cavalry decimated by ditches holding deadly spikes and caltrops which maimed the mighty destriers by bringing them to their knees; many rose in agony, but most never rose again. Aymer de Valence, Earl of Pembroke, had seized Edward's reins and steered him off the battlefield fearing for his sovereign's life. 'All is lost, sire.' Almost as he spoke the king's horse was speared by a lance and was severely wounded, its screams unearthly as it staggered in its death throes. A squire caught a riderless horse and helped the king to mount and flee the carnage.

In another part of the field Rufus Staveley roared, his voice cracked with the day's constant shouting of orders to his troops. 'Where are the bloody archers?' He sought his sergeant who lay among the piled-up bodies still whispering curses at the archers.

'If you help me escape this mountain of death I will tell you!' Pinned down by armour and dead troops Adam could not move until his powerful corporal began to pull at the bodies, eventually releasing the wounded sergeant. 'Douglas, damn his black soul, charged and routed them – they fled. Now come on, corporal, let you and me depart from this debacle with all speed and see if there are any of our men left.' Blood seeped from various wounds on both men's bodies but together they managed to escape the killing crews that were searching the field of dead for prizes and prisoners and slaying those they thought would bring neither gain nor fame.

Bruce's reputation grew both as a commander and a man of honour. He treated his noble prisoners with respect, releasing Ralph de Monthermer without ransom along with many others, but his most prized prisoner, Humphrey de Bohun, the Earl of Hereford, was exchanged for his wife, daughter and sister. The latter had been hung in a cage outside the castle walls at Roxburgh for years, suffering the same fate as the Countess of Buchan at Berwick.

Amongst those that escaped with their lives were the LeStrange kinsmen, but Eubolo had sustained a deep wound to his thigh. It was obvious that the loss of blood was endangering his life so Fulke, seeing all was lost, headed towards the safety of the north of England with his wounded cousin. When they finally reached Pontefract Eubolo was close to death and as he was carried into the infirmary Brother Vincent was sent for to perform the last rites.

The quiet figure of Simon the physician moved to stand beside Eubolo's moaning figure. He immediately stripped and bathed the ugly wound, then applied poultices and salve to aid healing using the methods taught to him by Ralph, his mentor. Somehow he managed to get Eubolo to swallow some mixture known only to a few and almost immediately the grey pallor was replaced by a pale, but healthier tone.

It was how Alice found Eubolo as she entered the infirmary on her daily visit. On learning of the devastating news from Bannockburn Alice had stayed with Joan Stapleton for a few days after they had learned of the tragic news from Stirlingshire that Joan had lost both her husband and a stepson in the battle. Alice returned to Pontefract knowing many wounded would head for the safety of those stout walls.

'Is he going to die?' Her face was filled with concern and fear as she asked the question of Simon.

'He is young and strong. I have given all the earthly medicines that I know... Now it is in God's hands.'

Alice reached across and touched Simon's arm. 'You have worked tirelessly and I thank you from my heart.'

Simon bowed. 'You have always shown both Master Ralph and myself nothing but kindness. He taught me his skills in God's name – I am merely his instrument.'

As he left Alice stooped and held Eubolo's hand. 'You must not die! You must not! You always had a bright smile and kind word at a time when both were as scarce as snow in summer.'

The prone figure moaned and Alice sat and held his hand until deep shadows crept across the bedcovers.

Matty whispered. 'You must come now, my lady, you have not eaten all day.'

Alice rose and smiled wanly. 'What sadness these wars bring. I hear that the Earl of Gloucester was slain and Robert Clifford was amongst a list of many. Oh, Matty, we must pray. Pray for forgiveness in destroying so many lives, and the poor horses – they say nearly all were killed. It grieves my heart.'

'Come now, lady, leave it to Brother Vincent to pray. They will bring you word if aught alters through the night.'

With heavy hearts the two women returned to Alice's chambers where a tray of tasty pies and fruits had been left out for them, accompanied by a jug of wine. Alice indicated for Matty to pour the wine and then invited her to join her.

'There is something else that bothers me about this bitter defeat.' She hesitated as Matty looked enquiringly at her. 'Lancaster!' Matty frowned. 'Don't you see? The king has been soundly beaten on the field of battle; his reputation is like a tattered standard, useless. Now Lancaster will be in the ascendancy. He and Warwick will hold him to account and woe betide anyone who opposes them. Gloucester was a mediator, respected by both men for all his lack of years – Valence does not hold as much sway with either of them. Hereford is a prisoner; who now will gainsay them?'

Matty nodded. All her troublesome dreams and premonitions all made sense.

Danger was the watchword, for with no one to stand against Lancaster and his allies her mistress stood completely alone and unprotected. What would become of Alice given this new turn of events; only God and time would answer that question.

Lancaster was eager to hammer home his advantage over his defeated cousin and travelled immediately to London, but Alice managed to convince him it was better for her to remain at Pontefract in case of further emergencies and for once even Robert Holland agreed to her proposal.

Daily she continued to visit Eubolo and the many wounded men. It became clear that the young nobleman was regaining his strength and some of his former spirits. However, as Simon explained, his wound had caused much damage to his muscles and sinews so he would forever have a pronounced limp. His first steps were with the aid of crutches, but gradually the crutches were replaced by a heavy stick and when Alice presented him with an ornately carved one with a silver top engraved with his family crest, Matty noted the tears in the young man's eyes.

It was the beginning of a close friendship between the countess and her former squire, and Matty was all too aware that on the part of the young Marcher lord his feelings ran much deeper than friendship. Although she was pleased to see the happiness their relationship obviously brought to both young people she was also aware that this new friendship would not go unnoticed by the earl's lackeys who would be only too pleased to report anything which might bring both praise and silver for their pains. There had been all too many occasions where Lancaster had used his heavy-handed methods against her beloved mistress.

During their many conversations Eubolo spoke eloquently of his love for his home of Shropshire and promised to show the countess his favourite haunts when she visited the region. Alice had little real hope of any such future visits, but it seemed to please him so much she allowed him to believe it to be a real possibility.

One evening, in late summer, as her favourite musician strummed a pretty medley of tunes, Alice walked out into her reinstated herb garden. The perfume of lavender hung in the air filling it with heady delight. The shadows crept across the beds and box hedges. Alice hummed along with the tunes and Matty and Luke Lytton, engaged in deep conversation as they stole a rare moment together, were so engrossed in each they failed to notice Alice disappear into the shadows, for neither made any move to join her.

'A magic evening is it not, my lady?'

Alice jumped at the words but smiled when she realised the identity of the speaker. 'Indeed, Master LeStrange.'

'I never thought I would get the smell of Bannockburn out of my nostrils but here, with you, it seems like a terrible nightmare.' He leaned heavily upon his stick, and quite without thinking Alice slipped her arm through his. Slowly they continued until they reached the arbour where she helped him to sit. Neither was aware of the watching gaze of Hugh de Freyne, who strained his eyes to see the identity of the couple below his vantage point high on the ramparts.

'How can I ever thank you, my dearest lady? I truly believe without your kindness and care I would have died.'

Alice looked deep into his eyes. 'Nonsense, the one you should thank is Master Simon. It was his skill that saved your life, not mine.'

Eubolo took her hand. 'It sometimes takes another kind of healing – love, which is far more potent than medicines.'

Alice drew her hand from his. 'Beware, Master LeStrange, do not misconstrue concern for anything deeper.'

'I know I have no right, but I *must* give voice to the feelings I have in my heart.'

'Pray say no more, for you will force me to avoid you in future – not for my sake but for your safety. Do you not realise the danger you place yourself in? And please say it matters not, think of me if not yourself.'

She rose and as she did so he pulled her down into his arms and kissed her with all the passion of his yearning. For Alice it was the first time she had ever been kissed with true emotion and she felt her body yield against his warm, young body. But she fought all her own pent-up longings and dragged herself out of his arms. She hurried back down the path, her silk cloak billowing out as she passed Luke and Matty, who noted how breathless she appeared, but she simply smiled and said, 'The perfume is quite heady, is it not?' and hurried back into the hall to the rest of the company, leaving the couple looking at each other in wonder.

Hugh de Freyne rushed down to the gardens but met with disappointment as the couple he had been watching were now nowhere to be seen. He entered the hall, but apart from Matty and Luke who were just wandering back all were seated or chatting quite unconcernedly.

Alice looked up at the burly figure. 'I do not believe you have been invited, my lord.'

'Merely seeing you were safe, my lady. I thought I saw someone in the garden.'

Alice stiffened but replied without hesitation, 'Pray have no fear, no one will come to any harm. There are armed guards at hand.' The company knew that de Freyne was Lancaster's man and had undoubtedly been given instructions to watch the countess closely. His dark gaze scanned the scene for the cloak, but a quick-thinking maid had hidden it behind a screen. The musician had ceased playing but at Alice's signal continued.

'Well, as you can see, all is well, so pray leave us to our diversions.'

Within days Alice made ready to leave Pontefract. She was sure now that Eubolo was well on the way to recovery and she knew if she remained she was in danger of following the dictates of her heart and that would be the path to death for both of them.

At the outset of her journey to the midlands the rains began and with each passing day the journey became more arduous and tiring. Roads turned to quagmire, the mud came above the horse's hocks and in some cases their knees, slowing their progress. Alice and her company passed fields of ruined crops and the dejected people who faced famine and the sight remained etched in all their minds.

Finally they reached Kenilworth and the exhausted party gave thanks to God for their safe arrival. Within days a large party headed by the Earls of Lancaster and Warwick arrived at the castle with a contingent of heavily armed guards. Alice smiled to herself; maybe her words of warning had made some impact upon Lancaster after all, for he only ever travelled abroad thus. At the banquet the following evening Alice sat between the two most powerful men in the country and still marvelled at how Warwick, whose reputation was as a learned and wise councillor, could have forged such a close alliance with Lancaster. She sat and listened to their discourse with intent; it appeared that they almost discounted the king in their discussion.

'Now he has to listen and be guided by us, for this defeat in Scotland serves only to emphasise his inadequacies in his leadership.' Lancaster's triumph was all too obvious and to Alice all the more dangerous in its naivety.

Warwick nodded and Alice found herself speaking out to the amazement of both men.

'Do you believe that the king will merely allow you to dictate his decisions now? Gaveston may not have been the evil councillor you judged him to be!' The room fell deathly silent as she continued. 'I accept he possessed a tongue as cruel as a whiplash but was he really the puppet-master?'

Lancaster thumped the table in his rage. 'Silence, madam, it is not your place to speak.'

But to Alice's complete amazement Warwick raise his hand. 'No, Lancaster, I for one would hear what your wife has to say. After all, is she not the daughter of one of the most respected councillors that ever served a nation. Lincoln's wisdom is sorely missed; maybe his daughter can enlighten us as to what he might have advised.'

The face of Thomas of Lancaster had darkened to a deep red but he held his tongue as Alice continued. 'Although Gaveston held the king's affections, did he really influence the king's major decisions? I know for certain he never requested an earldom; therefore was he the "evil councillor" he was accused of being when in fact he merely pricked men's pride? By bringing about his death you have incurred the long-lasting enmity of your king and whatever pardon he utters I for one have reason to believe that at some point he will seek his revenge upon those who had a hand in Gaveston's death. Surely, my lords, your loyalty should be to your country by supporting your king. The Scots are wreaking havoc on our borders and you in the king's council chambers are thereby aiding our country's enemies at this crucial time.'

Lancaster's patience snapped. 'Enough, enough, it is not for a mere woman to dictate the policies of the country to men. Pray sit silently for the rest of the meal.'

But Alice watched Warwick's face and knew that at least part of her words had made some impact on him and for that she was more than satisfied, knowing that she would be punished by Lancaster for her temerity. Later in the evening when Lancaster was engaged with his closest henchmen, Warwick turned to Alice.

'Lady, the king has made grave errors against the Ordinances and therefore must be bought to account; he is clearly not from the same mould as his sire.'

'I know this to be true, my lord, but to openly oppose the king surely cannot be a just act – quiet negotiations can serve far more effectively that open defiance. I know the Plantagenet characteristics, maybe better than most. Defiance will be a stumbling block to all your future dealings, whereas I know my father used humour and patience, and they often proved a far more effective weapon than belligerence.'

Warwick nodded. 'I know your husband can be somewhat high-handed at times.'

Alice smiled wryly. 'At all times, my lord.'

'Does he not listen to you?'

Alice chuckled. 'Never, my lord, we meet and speak only when absolutely necessary.'

'I find that a great pity as your father sired a wise child.'

Alice lowered her eyes, but a soft smile flickered around her lips.

That night as Alice prepared for bed, she noted Matty's tense expression. 'What ails you, Matty?'

'Oh, take no account of me, my lady.'

'Come, Matty, I know that look of old. There is something which is causing you great anxiety and I would learn of it!'

After a long hesitation Matty replied, her voice low, 'I saw Death hovering at the Earl of Warwick's shoulder.'

Alice looked askance at her lady-in-waiting. 'Maybe it was just a trick of the light.'

'Yes, of course, my lady, take no notice of my ramblings.'

Alice had cause to remember Matty's words when word came in the summer of the following year that Guy de Beauchamp, Earl of Warwick, was dead. There were mutterings that he had been poisoned by the king, but little credence was given to such rumours which were quickly squashed. However, Alice was not so certain. She of all people had warned of the king's revenge and she held the view that it could indeed be a possibility. This blow to the Ordainers would be felt most by Lancaster, for Warwick had been held in greater regard than the irascible Thomas Plantagenet, Earl of Lancaster.

The king now acted to curtail Lancaster's movements by issuing a summons for certain periods during that and the following year preventing Lancaster from travelling by horseback unless accompanied by royal guards, a situation that irked Lancaster greatly. He also had to deal with an uprising within his own lands in Lancashire. A number of knights whose lands had been taken in the unfair promotion of Robert de Holland had openly rebelled by looting castles and killing their occupants, so incensed were they at this unfair treatment by their liege lord Lancaster. Even Clitheroe Castle had fallen, and the enraged earl had retaliated by putting down the insurrection with all the vengeful brutality within his nature.

Alice had taken the news of the looting of Clitheroe Castle to heart as it was one her favourite residences. She had been suffering for months with indifferent health and this final piece of bad news caused her to take to her bed.

During this same period Isabella became aware that Edward was gaining new friendship amongst a few of the younger knights whose characters she was not wholly happy with; Roger Damory, lately created Earl of Oxford, and Hugh de Audley the Younger became his closest companions with a number of others on the periphery. Damory was handsome and dashing, but she judged him of little real intelligence, and de Audley was a much less flamboyant character. She liked not this new selection of friends.

At first Isabella saw nothing to fear, but she watched developments with keen interest. There was another lord in frequent attendance of late, one she instinctively disliked, Hugh Despencer the Younger, but as Edward also appeared to share her feelings about him she gave him little note. This was not so with his wife, Eleanor de Clare, one of the late Earl of Gloucester's sisters, who was also a favourite niece of the king. Isabella felt instinctively wary of this overly familiar relationship and became somewhat aggrieved towards the couple. Her instincts would be proved all too accurate over the coming years.

CHAPTER XVI

1316

Eleanor de Clare rolled lazily over and gently nibbled her husband's ear. 'You look somewhat put about, my lord.' She watched his expression.

'Damn Damory, he has the king's ear and I foresee he is manoeuvring to gain the title of Earl of Gloucester.'

Eleanor snuggled closer and ran her tongue round his ear. 'But Damory does not hold the king's long-standing affection, whereas I do! And…if you are clever, my lord, you can easily outwit the vain popinjay.' She smiled down at the prone figure of her husband Hugh Despencer. 'Also, as the eldest daughter, my claim to the Gloucester inheritance must take precedence, even though by law it should be shared three ways. As we both know there are some landholdings worth far more than others. I know my sisters, they can easily be brow-beaten. Therefore my claim must be the prime share, so why then not also include the title of Earl of Gloucester for my husband?'

Hugh Despencer smiled up at his wife. 'I swear I could not have chosen a better wife in all of England.'

Eleanor looked back at him, feigning a hurt expression. 'Only England, my lord?' He pulled her to him and they laughed, their merriment culminating in a passionate coupling, for even though Eleanor had born six children already to her lusty husband she found their love-making ever urgent, ever sensual, ever satisfying. They had learned each other's needs and desires and always aimed to fulfil the other's appetites, for theirs was a union of both physical and of acquisitive ambitions.

'It will be difficult to ignite any sort of friendship when he makes plain that he neither likes nor needs me!' Despencer dressed slowly, not calling for his manservant; these intimate moments were also a time of shared opinions and private discussions between him and his wife.

'Then find a way of making yourself indispensable, my darling. Times are difficult not only between the king and his magnates, but also between the king and his people, for they even blame him for the disastrous weather. Have you not heard the gossip about his careless mode of living and his choice of companions? Every facet of his life is watched by the court; his favourites attract jealousies like a magnet. All you need do is invent a little more scandal, strike a tinder at an appropriate moment, then watch Damory and the others' reputations go up in flames. Believe me, Edward will extricate himself from any bad gossip and let the blame fall on his favourites, thus leaving a gap at his side which I know you will find a way of filling most adequately.'

Eleanor stretched and smiled at her husband. 'Take heart, you have time and a powerful ally – your wife to assist with your…' she hesitated, then continued, '*our* advancement. My uncle is in need of an emotional crutch so make certain you are the one to take that role and relieve him of the onerous task of decision-making.' She smiled. 'It will therefore become an easy matter to forward our fortunes, will it not? Besides your father is well placed to see that no opportunity is missed to bring you into the king's company; it is then for you to make sure such opportunities bring forth positive results.' She smiled, her sharp features etched against the pale pillow. He nodded. Eleanor smiled and yawned.

'Mortimer has been defeated in Ireland, it will be easy to remind Edward of his failings and thereby prompt the beginnings of a split with that family, for are they not already the enemy of the Despencers? The plan? Divide and rule, my dear one, divide and rule.'

Hugh Despencer smiled. He liked his wife's plan. 'Oh, you may be assured I know this game and will become most adept at it, of that you can be certain, and together we will achieve our aims.' Eleanor felt satisfied with her strategy, little realising the deadly game she had incited – a game which would prove fatal for so many, including herself.

Totally unaware of the Despencers' plans, Alice de Lacy sat looking out over the bay near her home at Canford in Dorset, her horse pawing the ground as she watched the tide surge up the sandy shoreline. Even the inclement weather could not stop Alice riding out daily, and at moments like this, with the rain on her face and the wind teasing her riding habit, she experienced a moment of utter freedom. Here she could escape the constant wrangling between herself and Lancaster, who never missed an opportunity to slight her or make the lives of her servants as miserable as possible. She knew that he would learn that she had recovered sufficiently to ride out for at least an hour each day and would soon demand her return.

It was therefore no surprise to see Kit Cavendish waiting in her chamber upon her return.

'Ah, Master Cavendish, is the earl demanding my return?'

Kit smiled. He was a handsome young man and Alice wondered if he had a wife or mistress somewhere. 'No, my lady, I come on an entirely different mission, one where the message is by word of mouth and for your ears alone.'

Alice's eyes opened wide. 'Is this some intrigue you bring me?'

'No intrigue, my lady, although some may call it that, no doubt!'

'Then quickly put me out of my misery.'

Kit looked round to make sure they were not overheard. 'The Earl of Surrey wishes to inform you that the deteriorating relationship between you and your husband has come to the ears of a royal person who wishes to be your friend in this matter, in fact offers a possible means to extricate yourself from your current unhappy situation – that is, if you are willing.' Kit stood and watched as Alice listened, her lips slightly parted in amazement.

'Pray continue,' she said, then paused.

'When the right moment avails itself, would you be willing to be abducted and taken to Reigate where you would be under the protection of the Earl of Surrey. Once there, your husband could not touch you!'

Alice let out a long sigh before answering with a catch in her voice, 'Willing, of course I am willing. How much longer do you think I can withstand Lancaster's continuous abuse and humiliation? Daily my resistance wanes and my health suffers because of them.' She paused to regain her composure, adding softly, 'I have feared my resolve may weaken. Therefore, your news brings me renewed hope.' Then she continued, 'Of course, you realise it will mean you must also accompany me together with those that have been loyal to me these past years.'

A great smile lit his face. 'Oh, what a hardship, lady, when I would serve you with my life.'

Alice extended her hand, and he bowed and kissed it. 'Well said, Master Cavendish, but we must choose a propitious moment and not bring any suspicion on our plans before we are ready to move.'

The news the young messenger had delivered to Alice gave her a new lease of life; her health grew stronger daily. She no longer dreaded returning to Lancaster's household, for even if she had to make one last visit she now had the courage to withstand his barbs and insults. She would look on it as a penance for the sin of severing her marriage vows. Besides, the unpleasantries would last but a short duration.

The ravages of the constant rain were all too clear to see as they travelled along deeply rutted roads. The same sad scenes of poverty were evident wherever they passed those who had survived the brutal winter. Clawing hands, outstretched for whatever they could get. Alice felt moved by the gaunt, haggard children who appeared to her like walking skeletons. She distributed coins when she thought it safe to do so, often stopping at local churches to instruct the local clergy to buy food and clothing with her donations.

'Do you think God is punishing us?' Alice posed Brother Vincent the question upon her return to Kenilworth.

'If he is, he has his reasons.' The monk studied Alice's face at his reply.

'Pray what reasons could he have for causing the deaths of so many children?'

'Do not question his will, my lady, just pray for the strength to endure.'

Alice could not be reconciled with his words and found herself for the first time in her life questioning the will of her maker. 'War, pestilence, famine, the people who suffer the most are the ones who have the least control over events and decisions in the governance of the country. Surely God can see this sorry state of affairs which has little or nothing to do with the majority of his worshippers.'

Matty nodded in agreement, she knew how the scenes of famine they had witnessed along their route had touched her mistress's kind heart. When Alice retired that night, she lay lost in her own troubled thoughts, unable to sleep. She felt helpless; all her titles and wealth could achieve naught whilst she remained fettered to Lancaster who controlled both her fortune and her life. True, she had funded infirmaries in some areas, but not to the extent her conscience dictated. Her turbulent thoughts eventually subsided, allowing her to slip into an uneasy slumber.

The following day Lancaster rode back through the main gates at Kenilworth and the air of tension and uncertainty descended once more on the household. Even Robert Holland remained tight-lipped, for Lancaster's ire had fallen on him of late, as the uprising had been as a result of the resentment aroused by his receiving lands which had formerly been in Banastre hands.

One fact, however, favoured Lancaster. The king had recently given a formal pardon to those who had been involved in Gaveston's execution and the earl felt far easier and more self-satisfied than since the death of his erstwhile ally Warwick.

His wife, on the other hand, felt nothing but contempt for Lancaster and could not shake her deeply held feelings that Edward Plantagenet would at some point in time avenge the death of his friend.

When Thomas of Lancaster was in residence, all the female servants were in fear for their personal safety, for if they caught the eye of the lecherous nobleman few escaped his advances. Since Yolanda Artois had been sent back to France and married off, it left Lancaster free to cast his net of vice far and wide. However, some who were prepared to lose their reputation for financial gains flaunted themselves to find favour. What did it matter if they had a bastard or two as long as the reward was worth it: to those that pleased him he was known to give large purses of silver in return for his pleasure. Sadly, for those that resisted his advances, their future was dismissal, sometimes accompanied by rape and severe beatings. It was to Alice that many of those poor wretches came pleading for help and she was never found wanting in her charity.

It was for just such an act of kindness that Lancaster's truly brutal nature was revealed. On his discovery of Alice's part in helping one of his cast-offs, he brought down the full wrath of his vengeful nature – he not only beat the unfortunate maid but his wife too; so brutal was this beating that Alice could not leave her bed for many days. It was this final act of cruelty which prompted her to move and leave his household forever. If she stayed, she believed she would surely lose her life. As she lay, her slight body covered in bruises and lesions, she dictated a letter to Luke summoning her lawyers, Michael de Meledon and Walter Aleston, to act as her attorneys for a year.

By the time the two men arrived in late September, Alice had regained much of her composure, but both could see how fragile the countess looked and agreed she must seek rest to recover from her 'illness'. Neither man guessed at the reason for the state of the countess's health.

During the first week in October Alice and her small retinue were once more heading for Canford, and as she turned and looked back at the red sandstone walls of Kenilworth, she knew she would never again set foot there as long as it remained in Lancaster's hands. She looked at her small company of retainers, Noah, Gilbert, her falconer, Josh, her groom, Brother Vincent, Matty and Luke and a few men-at-arms, but in her heart she rejoiced she was a de Lacy and vowed never to suffer at Lancaster's hand again. The journey was arduous, and Alice's weakened state made for slow progress, but eventually they arrived at the welcoming sight of Canford Castle to await the plans for her 'abduction'.

CHAPTER XVII

1317

Isabella dropped her needlework into her lap. She could see Edward laughing at the antics of their eldest son who was playing with one of the hounds. It appeared that the dog did not know it was not human and the child did not know he was not a hound, so their play was quite magical in its innocence.

'I swear if aught happened to Jasper, our son would be heart-broken.' The king looked more relaxed than he had done for many months, although the news from Scotland and Ireland was hard to hear.

A frown played across Isabella's beautiful features and she chose to bring her concerns to the attention of her husband in this unguarded moment. 'You appear to have lost much of your dislike of the younger Despencer, my lord.'

Edward looked across at his wife and smiled. 'You know he has quite a fine wit under all that brashness. Besides, it pleases the Lady Eleanor that I no longer shun his company.'

Isabella picked up her skeins of silks, pulled a pale-green strand from the pile and handed it to her lady-in-waiting to thread. 'Pray have a care, my lord. To show too much favouritism only invites enmity and jealousy.'

'Oh, have no fear, he does not have all the qualities that Piers had and, besides, Damory is far more amusing, is he not?'

The queen knew that to pursue the topic further would only give cause for offence and that was indeed the last thing she wished to do, but it did not quell the mounting apprehension she experienced over the growing closeness of the younger Despencer. Why she had such feelings towards the son of her trusted advisor she could not explain; maybe it was linked to the fondness Edward showed towards his wife Eleanor, for that lady she also could not bring herself to trust. Eleanor de Clare was so unlike her sisters Margaret and Elizabeth; even in her looks it was only an occasional mannerism or tilt of the head that defined any kinship to her sisters at all.

For herself, Isabella felt more secure in her marriage now they had a second son, John of Eltham, who had been born the previous year. However, the relationship between Lancaster and the king was a real cause for concern and whilst the gap grew ever wider it left her husband's government divided, and such division within a country's ranks of magnates and clergy made for problems on all fronts. Isabella shivered – and this incessant rain did not help matters.

The continual raids of the Scots across the borders of the north only added to the king's problems. It had even been hinted that Lancaster could have made a deal with the Scottish king as his lands were never troubled by marauders. His brother, Henry of Lancaster, always insisted that this was merely because his brother could field a significant number of troops and thereby cause too much damage to the Scots. The truth was unknown, but Isabella felt that the growing tension between many of her husband's noblemen, which stemmed mainly from the quarrel with Lancaster, boded ill for the king. Until this family quarrel was resolved, or at least brought to a mutually agreeable level of understanding, then matters would only grow worse.

The main stumbling block to resolving the royal dispute was Damory, whom Lancaster blamed for the king's increasingly hostile attitude. He retaliated by sending raiding parties to a number of Damory's strongholds, causing mayhem and destruction. The king had been advised to take back many of the castles, thereby placing Damory under royal protection and making it more difficult for Lancaster to continue with his private war with the handsome Earl of Oxford.

Edward had added fuel to Lancaster's rage by awarding the hands in marriage of the de Clare sisters to his two closest favourites, Roger Damory and Hugh de Audley the Younger. By this act alone, he had raised their profile as well as their income. Margaret de Clare, widow of his dead friend Gaveston, he chose for the younger de Audley and Elizabeth, already twice widowed, he matched with Roger Damory. As the numbers of Edward's adherents grew, Lancaster on the other hand became ever more isolated, ever more furious, by virtue of his own personality. He did not easily attract friendships, which left him as the lone voice in opposition, even though Edward's supporters frequently had cause for complaint. However, Lancaster's great wealth and power did attract those intent on causing mischief to further their own ambitions.

Following her scandalous departure from her husband, Alice began to settle into life at Reigate Castle. Warenne had left many of his own servants to care for her, and she began to relax for the first time in her life. Now she was free from the pressure of her disastrous marriage, which had caused her so much pain. However, one member of her close attendants had left her service, not willingly, but by order of his bishop. Brother Vincent's recall arose from the fact that in the eyes of the Church, Alice had fallen from grace by breaking her marriage vows. It had been an awkward parting, for she knew the monk felt torn between his loyalty to her and the teachings of his Church.

'My lady, you know in my heart I do not judge your actions but must obey my orders. I will pray daily for your wellbeing and that you may find a way to be reconciled with your husband.'

Alice smiled at the thought, for they both knew that she would never return to Lancaster. Her decision had not been taken lightly.

'It grieves me that you now find yourself condemned by society and that your reputation is ruined.'

'Oh, Brother Vincent, do you think I care what name society calls me? I know who and what I am and have reached an age when I realise that it is my own conscience I must be true to. If I understand all you have taught me of the love of God, then I am sure he will forgive me, even if I have strayed from the teachings of the Church. After all, he forgave Mary Magdalen, and is it not true she remained loyal when many of the other apostles fled?' She continued in a lower tone. 'And I have never known another man but am unable to accept an intolerable life as Lancaster's wife.' He took her hands for an instant, then without further words made the sign of the cross over her and left.

She missed him greatly. Even though they had often disagreed on matters, they could argue and discuss all manner of topics without rancour, each respecting their differing views on life.

'You are lost in thought, lady!' Matty was busy picking up sheets of music as she spoke.

'You miss nothing, Matty.' Alice looked across at her beloved lady-in-waiting. 'I was merely thinking how Brother Vincent's presence is missed.'

'He could be a prickly pear on occasions but for all that he was an honest priest.'

'Matty, are you judging God's messenger?'

'He is a man first whatever vocation he follows, and human nature has often been the downfall of men, even men of the cloth.' Alice could not argue with that. She had witnessed the ambitions of the clergy, which had frequently brought about arguments between Church and state. Even now she learned that the see at Durham was being contested by Rome, the king and the queen, all supporting their different candidates for the position. Now such matters were no longer her concern. She was living in comparative seclusion and she found it suited her well.

However, not everyone shunned the countess, for she received letters of invitation from a number of people, and two in particular had been received with great pleasure. One was from her former stepmother, Joan Martin, now married to Nicholas de Audley, and the second from Eubolo LeStrange who had returned to his home in the Welsh Marches.

On meeting her stepmother again the two fell into a much easier relationship than when Joan had been married to Alice's father, the Earl of Lincoln, and Alice had the rare pleasure of seeing a family in harmony. Although Nicholas de Audley was a nobleman, he neither held an important office nor was of any notable wealth, but to Alice their wealth lay in the happiness of the family life they shared.

Joan also noted the difference in Alice, for she looked so much younger and her health appeared much recovered. It was a joy to watch as she played happily with Joan's young children.

'You should have had children of your own,' Joan said one afternoon as Alice sat nursing the youngest child who lay sleeping in her arms.

'I am afraid I shall never bear a child of my own and have reconciled myself to that. It is God's will and that is how I must accept it! Besides, can you imagine Lancaster and me agreeing on anything to do with a child? No! Married to such a man I am quite content that I have thwarted him in at least one important aspect of his lineage. His brother is by far the more worthy of title of earl and had he been chosen as my husband...' Her words trailed off and Joan pressed the subject no further.

A few weeks later, Joan and Nicholas began making plans to travel to another of their properties, whilst Alice made ready with her small retinue to head towards Shropshire and the seat of the LeStrange family. Eubolo had sent an invitation for her to stay at his mother's favourite residence, Cheswardine Castle.

The time spent at Cheswardine was a truly special time in Alice's life and although Eubolo had tried on a number of occasions to voice his true feelings, she always refused to listen.

'My dearest lord, we both know that at this time it is inappropriate to venture into a realm of emotion. I am in no position to receive or return such feelings,' she hesitated, then continued, 'especially of affection.' His crestfallen face had touched her heart and she added gently, 'Suffice it to know that having your love gives me strength. There are too many enemies around us waiting to bring us down and I for one would never wish you or your family to suffer through any rash act on my part.'

'But does that mean...' he let out a slow sigh, 'that you...'

Alice shook her head. 'Enough! Pray, say no more at this time, then should you meet someone who is free...?'

'I will love you every day I have left on earth and if...' Alice reached up and touched his lips. He kissed the tips of her fingers, then they continued their walk.

This sweet interlude passed all too quickly and Alice knew she could not linger there, although she understood Eubolo's mother's reasons for making Cheswardine her favourite home. There was indeed a peace and tranquillity about the woods and pools. The farmland was grazed by healthy, plump cattle who had so far escaped the dreadful murrain, which was spreading rapidly through the country. Many thought it was the result of all the rainfall and poor crops of the past two years. Some, that it was God's punishment for all the wars and sins of the world. Some blamed cattle which had been brought across from France. Whatever the true cause of the catastrophe, it was yet another factor that was adding to the devastation of England's people.

As Alice rode back towards Reigate she found herself stopping at a priory run by the poor nuns of St Agnes and there she prayed for guidance to show her the path that would bring her back into God's good grace. Whilst at the priory, a messenger who had been attacked on his road south was brought into the infirmary. As one of the nuns treated his bloody wounds, Alice learned he had been carrying word of events on the Borders. She listened as the luckless man told of the terrible attack which had taken place, little knowing he was talking to the Countess of Lancaster. The details of the raid near York had involved many of the clergy who had faced a savage army of Scots, only to be slain. The nuns were deeply shocked on hearing this outrageous news and immediately offered up prayers for the fallen. But it was what he said next that affected Alice most. In a weak, cracked voice he continued, 'That Earl of Lancaster deserted the king and returned to his own lands in the north, even though so many churchmen had been killed.' He looked across at Alice. 'What's it all coming to, my lady, when our own knights and earls won't support their liege lord?'

'I know not, sir, but as you say it leaves England in a sorry state.'

That night Alice lay awake mulling over the news and she silently wept. What would her beloved father have done in such a situation? And with ravaging thoughts tearing through her mind she finally slept in a fitful, dream-filled sleep.

CHAPTER XVIII

Autumn 1319

Over the past few years matters of state had grown increasingly worse, but as yet had had little effect upon Alice's life at Reigate. However, news began to arrive from the north that Berwick had fallen and John de Warenne, Earl of Surrey, had been summoned by the king with all available men to reinforce the army in an effort to regain the stronghold, which had been in English hands since 1296.

Alice decided it was time to leave and return to her own castle in Dorset and trust that Lancaster would not trouble her there. He had to date taken no steps to urge her return. On their journey west they witnessed an air of gloom and fear in every town, village, hamlet and croft. The party continued in almost complete silence for there were no words of comfort. It was, therefore, with a feeling of huge relief that they finally arrived at Canford.

A messenger from the Earl of Surrey arrived conveying his apologies for only sending a handful of men-at-arms to protect Alice, but that his venture on the Borders had had to take precedence and he did not believe she was now in any imminent danger from Lancaster.

Over the coming weeks, Alice gleaned more snippets of information, which began to give cause for anxiety. The king's new favourite, Hugh Despencer the Younger, now held the power of veto over all who wished to petition the king or indeed have any discourse with him whatsoever. Even the queen was under the ever-watchful gaze of Despencer's wife Eleanor.

'The fox and the vixen!' Matty looked up at Alice noting the venom with which she spoke.

'Of whom do you speak, my lady?'

'Why the scheming Despencers, of course. As I recall, Edward had no liking for Eleanor's husband, so how have his fortunes changed so rapidly?'

'It is no good fretting over matters which you cannot influence.' Matty was busily spinning some fine wool, and as she worked her shadow reflected on the solar walls.

'You are right as ever but it causes me great concern at how unlike his father the king is in his close associates, none of whom appear to be steering him on a safe course, it would seem. Men like Despencer are avaricious and methinks he desires the title of Earl of Gloucester.'

'Then all we can do, my lady, is offer up our prayers and hope that the future holds the key to better times.'

Alice looked at her beloved lady-in-waiting, who meant so much to her: companion, nursemaid and friend. She smiled wryly at the statement. 'Well, we will have to seek the local priest to come more frequently as the Church refuses to allow us our own confessor these days. The Church is ruled by men; therefore I am branded a daughter of Eve and must bear the weight of her sin.'

'Eve has much to answer for!' Matty grinned as she spoke.

Whilst Alice and her household awaited further news from the north, matters in the region deteriorated even more and the king turned ever more frequently to Despencer for advice and guidance. He felt beleaguered and irritated, especially with his cousin Lancaster. Hugh Despencer never lost an opportunity to pour venom into the king's ear with regard to the recalcitrant earl. However, the king knew that whilst his favourite and his royal cousin were at odds Scotland took second place, and with the Scottish raids becoming ever bolder he began to take steps to bring about a reconciliation with all those who opposed him, and at the forefront was Lancaster.

Many weeks of negotiations finally ended with the two Plantagenets arranging a meeting near Northampton so they could face each other with their grievances. On his part, the king was prepared to concede many of Lancaster's demands in order to bring the might and wealth of the earl under his command. Lancaster, on the other hand, saw a perfect opportunity to insist that the favourites he so detested should be sent from court in order for him to feel 'safe', as he accused them of endangering his life.

Edward reluctantly agreed and after a ceremony where all the most important and powerful magnates and prelates signed the document which became known as 'the Treaty of Leake', peace was finally brought.

Previously Lancaster's continual absences had disrupted so many of the king's plans that this treaty was viewed with satisfaction. However, it meant that many who had legitimate grievances against Lancaster were forced to accept terms, which proved hard to bear. One who found it most difficult was John de Warenne, Earl of Surrey, who grudgingly bent his knee to Lancaster, ostensibly ending their quarrel.

However, Warenne was hardly likely to let this public show of reconciliation alter any of his personal feelings towards Lancaster. After Warenne's alleged part in the 'abduction' of Alice de Lacy, Lancaster had invaded lands owned by him, including the castles of Sandal and Conisburgh which had both suffered considerable damage. Therefore, it was unlikely Warenne would meekly accept this imposed peace for long but would wait for an opportune moment to take his revenge.

As for Damory, who had also lost lands and castles to Lancaster, would he also stay his hand for long? It remained to be seen. This left Hugh de Audley the Younger, William Montacute and the Despencers; how would they react in the future? Would this agreement prove strong enough to keep the ambitions of England's most powerful noblemen in check?

All appeared set to focus once more on the enemy, Scotland, and the forthcoming siege of Berwick. Lancaster, true to character, merely made a show of arms, for none of his men appeared to be actively engaged in any fighting. The younger Despencer gloatingly pointed out the fact to the king and any who would listen. It was still rumoured that Lancaster was in league with the Scots and had paid large sums of silver to avert any attacks on his northern lands. Whether there was a grain of truth in this was uncertain, or it was merely down to the fact that the Scots were averse to confronting a powerful earl, knowing the might of men he had under his command. They were not foolhardy enough to lose men on lost causes.

Like so many previous English offensives, it went badly for the royal forces. The siege was abandoned yet again, leaving a bitter taste of defeat and frustration in the mouth of the king. The disgruntled army marched back south with only sick, wounded men and disheartened troops to show for their efforts.

It gave Despencer time to turn his attention to the lands he coveted in the Gower in the Welsh Marches, but the move was vigorously repelled by the Earl of Hereford, the lords Mortimer and Roger Damory, who also held lands by right of his wife.

However, the king upheld the claims of Despencer as he was now totally in thrall to his scheming favourite. It was only when his trusted councillors, the Earl of Pembroke and Bartholomew Badlesmere, voiced their concerns, echoed by Isabella, about the worsening situation that if Edward failed to listen to reason it would lead to open rebellion and civil war.

This was not a position the king had envisaged and he came unwillingly to listen to the growing list of complaints against his favourite. He resented his wishes being thwarted and would not easily forgive those that opposed him. He conveniently forgot that those who were now ranged against him had once been loyal adherents to the Crown and had stood fast against the Welsh in past decades. He faced the powerful Marcher lords with a heavy heart, finally agreeing to send the Despencers from his court. The elder went to the Continent and the younger took to the seas, where he instantly became the scourge of the Channel as a pirate, his victims targeted indiscriminately in his illegal venture.

The news of the failed siege of Berwick reached Alice sometime afterwards and, upon learning of Lancaster's part in failing to send troops, voiced her fears to Matty.

'The earl is running true to form, I fear.' She waited for Matty's reaction, but when none was forthcoming continued, 'If ever a man had his fate etched upon his face it is Lancaster. Selfish, arrogant, brutish with little or no grasp of a dangerous situation, and the king is just as stubborn and unrelenting as any of that family.' She shrugged her shoulders, then continued, 'I can foresee only one end to the situation – civil war – and where will that leave the people of England? My father always said the bloodiest war was a civil one; family against family, brother against brother.' She hid her face in her hands.

Matty put down her needlework and folded Alice in her arms. 'Come now, sweeting, 'tis no good upsetting yourself, men will be men, kings will be kings for good or ill, and we, as subjects, must submit to the inevitable order of things.' The two women stood for a while in a comforting embrace until a knock at the door broke the moment.

Kit Cavendish came and dropped to his knee before Alice, his handsome face and clothes stained with the dirt from his long hours in the saddle. 'Lady, I fear I bring bad tidings. Lady Maud, your sister-in-law, is dead.'

Both women made the sign of the cross. Alice spoke softly, 'Poor Henry, just at a time when he will need all the comfort and support to withstand the troubles created by his brother's mindless actions and the Despencers' unquenchable ambitions.' She held out her hand and Kit kissed it. 'Pray dine with us tonight, Kit.' He bowed and murmured his thanks; it was not often a messenger got to sit with nobility, but then the Countess of Lancaster was like no other gentlewoman he had ever encountered.

As Alice had rightly predicted, England's fortunes were about to sink even lower. The king was becoming ever more estranged from his queen and magnates, but for the meantime all she could do was wait for events to unfold. Kit Cavendish played a major role in keeping the countess abreast of the turbulent times. He covered many dangerous miles and often only escaped harm by the fleet-footedness of his horses.

It was whilst he was in Ludlow gleaning news and gossip about events in the Marches that he met and fell in love with a merchant's daughter, Blanche. When later he knelt before Alice to request her permission for his marriage, he received not only her blessing but also a magnificent bedcover as a wedding gift.

'Tell me more about your merchant's daughter.'

Kit smiled shyly; it had happened so suddenly that he could scarce believe it. 'Well...she is the second daughter of Edwin Merriman who lives some two leagues from Ludlow, and...' he hesitated, 'he wishes me to join him.'

'And is that what you want?' Alice studied Kit's expression as he answered.

'I think it would suit me as I would still be riding across the country and would be in an even better position to gain information from a higher level of society.'

Alice smiled. 'Oh, Kit, I absolve you from any duties to me and am happy for your advancement. I hope Edwin Merriman appreciates his good fortune in gaining such a capable son-in-law.'

Kit smiled. 'But I shall always be at your service, my lady, whatever and wherever I am.'

True to his word, Kit did keep Alice informed, but the news was not easy to listen to. The Despencers returned to bring about further mayhem with their persistent greed and the king did naught to gainsay their ambitions. It left the lords of the Marches so angry they used force of arms to resist the younger Despencer.

Alice knew events were playing right into the hands of Thomas of Lancaster and if he had an ounce of wit, he would use them to his advantage. Sadly, she also realised logic was used but infrequently and his pride, therefore, would serve against him. Such was the predicament that now prevailed in England. Plantagenet against Plantagenet, magnates in open opposition to their king. Meanwhile the Scots were raiding the Borders with little or no resistance from the English. In her heart Alice felt the outcome would be civil war and she dreaded that day dawning.

CHAPTER XIX

Pontefract
March 1322

'Holland, where is Holland?' The voice of Thomas of Lancaster was hollow and harsh.

His squire bowed his head, afraid that what he was about to tell his master would earn him a blow. 'He has deserted, my lord earl.'

The look that crossed the earl's features was terrifying as the colour drained away, to leave a mask-like visage. 'How many others?'

'Too many to be accurate, my lord.'

'Hereford?'

'He is mustering men and weapons as too is the lord Damory.'

'At least not all are craven cowards. If I survive this day, I swear I will hunt them down like the wolf hunts its prey, rip out their cowardly hearts and give them to hold in their dying minutes.' His squire bowed, knowing his master did not utter idle threats.

'What are you waiting for, fool, summon my charger and fetch me my armour.'

Glad to to be leaving the earl's presence even for a short time, the youth darted out of the chamber and did his master's bidding, thankful to have escaped injury at least for the moment.

Thomas of Lancaster went to his chapel whilst he awaited the arrival of his armour and knelt to pray before his dour-faced priest, who muttered a few prayers and made the sign of the cross in benediction. 'May the Lord be with you.'

As Thomas left, there was little room for divine prayers within his heart for he hated the man he knew had brought about this situation, the snake Despencer. Lancaster cursed him vehemently as he prepared for the day's battle.

What followed was utter defeat for Lancaster, and the sixteenth of March was a day which demonstrated the viciousness of the

Plantagenet king and his ever-present advisor and favourite, Hugh Despencer the Younger. The battle was bloody and intense and was finally won for the Crown by Thomas's erstwhile adherent, Andrew Harclay, who used more lightly armed hobelars rather than ponderous heavy cavalry, much as the Scots had done at Bannockburn. The Earl of Hereford was killed by a pikeman hiding beneath the bridge at Boroughbridge, who skewered both the earl and his charger. Damory received serious wounds after fighting valiantly, but managed to escape the final carnage. As for the once-powerful Earl of Lancaster, he was dragged past jeering crowds of troops to be imprisoned in his own castle at Pontefract. Nothing was left of his former overwhelming pride, as he was reduced to a pathetic figure, besmirched, bloody and downcast.

Alice learned of Lancaster's defeat from swift-riding messengers who were spreading the news of the king's great victory. She also heard an account of the trial at which Lancaster was not allowed to speak in his own defence. Afterwards he was roughly hustled from the court to the place of his execution, then dragged behind one of the poorest nags that could be found. Such was the ignominious end for a man who had shown scant regard towards anyone throughout his lifetime. Apparently even the pleas of mercy by the queen had gone unheeded by Edward. The only concession to his status was the manner of his execution, commuted to beheading, but even that was a botched and gruesome affair. Badlesmere and the others were hung, drawn and quartered in a brutal show of vengeance by the king.

The wounded Damory escaped to reach his wife Elizabeth de Clare, the king's niece, who pleaded for his life, but he died soon after from his wounds, leaving her a widow for the third time. The aftermath of the civil war was to be felt for years to come by many families throughout the land. Despencer and the king moved swiftly to seize lands and titles, sparing lives only after receiving vast sums of silver. Their acts of avarice left a bitter taste for revenge in the mouths of many and the king's reputation suffered even further as a result, whilst hatred towards the Despencers increased tenfold as their reputation for savagery grew apace. Despencer now focused on the surviving wives and children of those who had dared to oppose the king.

Alice was just one of many women who found themselves arrested and imprisoned, some to be confined within the walls of their own castles. Like some common prisoner, Alice was escorted to one of York's many prisons, where she was locked within its dank, forbidding walls. She was without servants, edible food and a change of clean linen and was treated with the utmost disrespect. The realisation that she stood in certain danger of losing her life quickly dawned.

Alone, hungry and filled with gnawing pangs of fear, Alice faced the most dangerous period of her life. The word heresy had been threatened and the penalty for that crime was death by burning. She felt it somewhat ironic that she was being accused of Lancaster's treason, when she had so vehemently spoken out against it. Her only comfort was the rosary of moonstones, the gift from her long-dead father, which she had somehow managed to hide from her captors. Daily she prayed not only to God but also to her father to deliver her from this evil place and send her the courage to overcome these earthly perils.

Only the silver that Matty managed to secrete to a guard allowed any outside contact at all, but he was fearful of any further favours, other than the occasional message or note. On one such message was scribbled: '*Give them whatever lands and titles they want, none is worth losing your life for! You are in our prayers. God go with you!*' It left Alice wondering whether she would be given any option or just summarily taken out and put to death, for justice ruled nowadays in favour of the king and Despencer. The fear of poisoning made it easy for her to refuse the poor fare she was offered.

Strangely, it was the rapidly deteriorating situation in France which served as Alice's saviour as Despencer's attention was, at least for the time being, diverted from his current activities in England, which acted in Alice's favour. Therefore, after many weeks of maltreatment, the Countess of Lincoln found herself sitting opposite a serious-faced cleric who clutched a sheaf of documents.

'I have been sent to obtain your signature upon the transfer of lands and titles to the Crown. I suggest you sign immediately; it will bode ill for you should you show any signs of resisting the royal request.'

Alice looked across to the officious cleric and replied softly, 'You should at least show me the civility of addressing me as Countess of Lincoln and Salisbury. Or is the lack of courtesy a foretaste of the future?' She stared steadily across the rough-hewn trestle.

The scribe cleared his throat. 'Neither your high-born station nor any courtesy I afford you will alter the fact that if you do not sign, your position will grow ever worse. Believe me, madam, the Lord Despencer and the king will brook no refusal.'

Alice rose slowly and walked round the chamber, then turned and spoke to the cleric who she could see was becoming more discomforted by the minute. 'Soo!' She let the word slide along the walls and round the chilly chamber. 'I note in which order you show your deference. Have a care, master cleric, the wheel of fortune has the inevitable habit of turning at times all too quickly. I have learned to value what truly matters in life, my own self-respect and my adherence to God.' She had twisted the smooth beads of her rosary around her fingers. She paused before continuing, 'As to the ambitions of men and kings I care not one jot. Pass the accursed documents and leave me in peace.'

As the quill scratched across the parchment Alice wondered what her beloved father's reactions would have been watching her sign away so much of the Lincoln lands and wealth he had fought and served his country for, but Despencer's greed knew no bounds and she would never have been allowed to enjoy them. Better to live without fear of reprisals than to die and lose everything.

Hastily the cleric sanded the signatures, rolled up the signed scrolls and made his exit. Within the week she was released, glad to be reunited with Matty, Luke, Noah and the rest of her faithful servants. Weak and frail she made the short journey to a pleasant inn where she bathed, changed her clothing and sipped a nourishing beverage. She was eager now to catch up with news from the outside world and happy to have Matty once more in charge of her wellbeing.

'Oh, by the by, that young Marcher lord has been trying to gain knowledge of your whereabouts, you know, the one who had been badly wounded.'

Alice's heart skipped a beat. 'Eubolo LeStrange?'

'Aye, that's the one.' Matty smiled knowingly. 'Time has not dimmed his loyalty 'twould seem!'

Alice shook her head. 'It is good to know I have not been completely forgotten.'

She also learned that Luke had written to the Bishop of Lincoln, Henry of Lancaster and the Earl of Surrey acquainting them with her situation and requesting their aid. But matters between the king and his magnates had never been worse, so they found themselves helpless to take any action, knowing their own positions were precarious at this time.

During the second week of her stay, Alice's strength slowly began to return and she started to make plans to go to one of the small estates which were not included in her dowry. Alice gave a silent prayer of thanks to her mother who had made her current position more bearable, for she would not starve. However, the solution to her immediate future came in the form of the young lord from the Marches, Eubolo LeStrange, who invited Alice and her retainers to one of his family's castles in Shropshire.

Matty had no doubt whatsoever that Eubolo loved Alice, but was not so certain that the feelings were reciprocated. However, as the small party made their way slowly towards the midlands Matty noted the glances between the two and began to have hope Alice might have finally found the love she had always wished for her. At last, the future looked as though it could hold a promise of better things to come.

The king, on the other hand, found precious little time to enjoy his victory over his erring cousin as matters in France gave him cause for great concern. Charles, king of France, was demanding Edward's vows of fealty for lands and titles he held in France and Gascony. Lancaster's death had cast a long shadow of resentment throughout the English nobility and when the Church added its voice to the growing swell of unrest, a feeling of consternation descended on Edward and his hated councillor Despencer. The king was fearful that if he left England the magnates would rise up and overthrow his favourite.

For months, Edward made excuses until the French king's patience finally ended and he demanded the English king give up the French territories and titles or face armed conflict. The situation gave Isabella the opportunity she had been waiting for, cleverly offering to play mediator with her brother on her husband's behalf. Despencer, desperate not to be left alone in England, eagerly agreed to this course of action. Neither realised how foolishly they had played right into Isabella's hands. As arrangements were made for her departure, the queen gave no indication what was really in her heart – all she wished to do was to escape the Despencers' constant control.

Isabella had already experienced the heavy hand of the Despencer policies, for when the French situation had originated the man she now viewed as her enemy, Despencer the Younger, had urged the king to expel all French citizens, which included the queen's own retainers, people who had served her all the years she had been in England. The queen was not about to submit meekly to the dictates of a man whom she considered no better than a lackey. She resented the hold Despencer had over Edward; he had even curtailed her visits to the king and had forbidden her access to her own children, placing the younger ones in the care of his wife Eleanor who already acted as his spy, watching her every move.

Once in France, Isabella planned to appeal to both her brother and the pope to order Despencer's dismissal from her husband's side. She had little idea at this juncture exactly how momentously events would unfold once she was in the country of her birth, only that she would have a chance to seek help from her brother Charles, king of France, and the pope.

CHAPTER XX

Ellesmere Castle
1324

The chapel felt cool and chill. Matty shivered – outside the sun was shining and the air was hot and heavy as a summer storm brewed. There were only a handful of people gathered for the ceremony. Nevertheless it was a truly momentous occasion. Alice de Lacy, Countess of Lincoln and Salisbury, and Eubolo LeStrange stood before the altar and made their vows of marriage.

Alice wore a kirtle of dove-grey silk and a surcoat of Persian-blue Italian velvet; her headdress of diamonds, sapphires and pearls sparkled as she moved, and Matty thought she had never seen Alice look lovelier or happier in all the years she had spent in her service. At last, the long, empty years which had been void of love for Alice were forever banished. Tears of joy filled Matty's eyes and she looked across at the tall figure of Luke Lytton who stared straight ahead. She remembered the time when they had planned to marry but because of circumstances surrounding their mistress Matty had persistently refused to name a day. She knew their time had sadly passed. Now the two were close friends, but the physical attraction through the years had waned. Matty's loyalty was and always would be to Alice and she had feared that once married she would be constrained by her marriage vows.

The weeks after their wedding Alice and Eubolo spent exploring the lands of the LeStrange family who had long since settled in Shropshire. Alice found the area of Shropshire and the Welsh Marches much to her liking. The bare, windswept moors of Lancashire and Yorkshire that she so loved now vied with rich, majestic hills, glistening meres, and rivers which varied from lazy, meandering courses to surging, urgent waters racing towards their distant destination. Colourful plains stretched to the foothills where the creamy-coloured sheep cropped the rich pastures.

The couple had been offered Ellesmere Castle as their home and Alice enjoyed the close proximity of the serene meres, which as the autumn approached were often veiled in a soft haze providing a mystical aura. Events of the outside world they held at bay for as long as possible, but travelling monks, troubadours and minstrels brought current news, which was to have a far-reaching effect upon the couple.

Kit had ridden over from Ludlow himself, detailing the dramatic escape from the Tower of London of Roger Mortimer of Wigmore. The king had issued an immediate warrant of hue and cry, added to which was a large bounty for his capture. All in vain – Mortimer was now safely in France, his exact location as yet unknown, but his youngest son Geoffrey had estates there, as did many of his mother's kinsmen.

News also arrived of the death of Aymer de Valence, Earl of Pembroke, who had so often been the moderating voice in the constant wrangling between the king and his magnates. This was sad tidings indeed as his voice of reason would be sadly missed.

However, Alice was delighted to see Kit and keen to learn of his wife and new life and she plied him with questions on how they fared in these difficult times. He told her of their expanding wool trade, which brought both prosperity and a growing reputation.

'No doubt your father-in-law has come to value your addition to his business.'

'Indeed, and I consider myself most fortunate that my wife is the sweetest creature alive.'

Alice smiled. 'You deserve good fortune, Kit, and may God keep you and your family safe and well.'

Whilst Alice and Eubolo enjoyed their new situation as man and wife, the king and Despencer faced ever-mounting problems both at home and abroad. The queen was preparing for her imminent departure to France in an effort to avert impending hostilities with England. During this period Alice learned that her brother-in-law, Henry of Lancaster, had been made Earl of Leicester and that matters between the king, his nobles and members of the Church were deteriorating daily. Already Pembroke's death was being felt, his steadying influence now totally replaced by the rapacious rule of the hated Despencers. But the intrigues of the court cast but a pale shadow over the LeStrange household as Alice and Eubolo faced the uncertain future together.

After the merriment and amusements of Yuletide had passed, the year 1325 moved towards spring. A party of merchants, who had recently returned from Flanders, stopped over on their homeward journey and spoke of Isabella's visit to France. Apparently, upon her arrival she had been feted and cheered, and appeared to be successfully fulfilling the role to which she had been entrusted. However, the queen had stunned many when she had publicly denounced Despencer by donning widow's weeds, emphasising what she saw as her diminished situation.

'I wonder how Despencer and the king received this news,' Alice said artlessly. Secretly she applauded Isabella's open opposition to the hated Despencers.

The scandal grew even greater when a musician, who had recently entertained the king at court, revealed the queen was now refusing to return to England, causing consternation amongst the royal party, especially for the Despencers, who were becoming ever more fearful of their position. The king and his favourite were always mindful that Mortimer was also on the Continent. When he learned of Isabella's stand against her husband, he would no doubt seek to cause mischief for them.

Whatever impending troubles lurked in the future for the king and his favourite, Alice de Lacy had never felt happier. Eubolo was everything she had ever wished for in a husband; he was witty, loving and kind, and sought to find ways of pleasing her every day. The haunting fear from her former life vanished as she revelled in this newly found freedom. No longer did she come under constant scrutiny or feel constrained in spontaneous speech. Matty frequently heard laughter coming from the couple's chambers, and Eubolo often teased Matty, but always ended the prank with a kiss on her cheek.

However, the halcyon days were soon to change with a letter from Fulke LeStrange, who was presently serving in Gascony, warning that Isabella had indeed formed an alliance with Mortimer and that Fulke had heard rumours they intended to invade England as soon as they had gathered enough troops, horses and equipment. The matter had become ever more critical when the king was persuaded to send his eldest son to France to pay homage to King Charles for the lands in France and Gascony which Edward had recently bestowed on his son in an effort to avoid open warfare with his brother-in-law.

As Alice and Eubolo sat before a merry fire one evening she posed the question that had been plaguing her mind since they had read Fulke's letter. 'So where does your allegiance lie, my lord, with the king or the queen?'

Eubolo was arranging the chess pieces on the leather gaming board. 'The LeStrange family have ever been loyal to the Crown but…' he hesitated and stopped his task, 'to tell you the truth, my love, I have a head that says the king has allowed the Despencers too much power which has been both misused and abused. The queen, on the other hand, has always, until this unholy relationship betwixt the king and Despencer, proved a good and honourable consort. Therefore, I find myself in a position which lies between my head and my heart.' He smiled wryly. 'I must leave the decision to the head of the family and see which way they will act. So let us not waste a pleasant evening by worrying over events which have not yet happened and play a game we can enjoy.'

Alice was somewhat discomforted by the fact that Eubolo had not asked for her opinion, something she had thought would have been a natural thing for him to do. Was this how a younger member of a family acted or was it just an easier option not to take responsibility? As she sat down to play the game of chess, her mind pondered the question.

Later that night, when she knew Eubolo slept, Alice rose from their large bed and silently sought her own chambers. She sat looking into the dying embers of the fire when she heard someone enter the room; it was Matty.

'What ails you, my lady?'

'Oh, do not fret, Matty, I am not ill, just at odds with my emotions.'

'A fear shared is a fear defeated,' said Matty, as she came and sat before the fire.

'I looked to this union with Eubolo as a complete sharing of all of life's issues, now I find that I am treated as a nobody by the one person I thought would never do that!'

Matty sat silently for a while before answering her mistress. 'Lord Eubolo is not totally in control of his own destiny. He must comply with his elder brother or cause a family rift, something he would avoid at all costs, methinks. His motives may have been completely innocent. He knows how your health suffered after York and maybe wanted to spare you any untoward distress.' She watched Alice's expression, then continued. 'Talk to him and tell him how you feel, you may have judged him guilty where no guilt lies.'

'My dearest Matty, you should be one of the king's ministers, for your sound good sense always prevails. As you so rightly say I have jumped to a conclusion which may prove totally unfounded. Now we shall have a sip of wine and seek our beds.'

The following day Alice spoke to Eubolo about her fears and he quickly managed to dispel her doubts, for it was as Matty had predicted, he had only remained silent to save Alice any fears she may have held, and so the two regained their harmonious relationship.

Rumours and gossip abounded regarding Isabella's efforts to gain the pope's support in ordering the removal of the hated Despencer from Edward's side. It coincided with the arrival of news that the king had also written to Rome requesting the pope's intercession. However, his request also contained a plea ordering Isabella's immediate return to England. Therefore, the situation remained in stalemate until the fateful news that the queen was indeed enlisting troops and equipment in readiness for an invasion of England. The roads were abuzz with messengers carrying letters to and from the Continent.

CHAPTER XXI

1326

Kit Cavendish galloped into the courtyard at Ellesmere, his dishevelled appearance enough to advertise his urgency. He was ushered into the chamber where Alice and Eubolo were poring over a pile of documents. Without any preamble he uttered the words Alice had been dreading. 'The queen and Mortimer have landed in Suffolk – the king ordered the Earl of Lancaster to intercept them. Instead, he joined the queen's party, as have many – in fact, most of the nobles on their route. I have also learned that orders have also been issued for you and your brothers to join the earl at all speed.' Kit looked at Eubolo to see his reaction before continuing, 'The most recent news is that the king and Lord Despencer have fled to Wales.' Kit knew this information was of great significance to the couple.

Alice and Eubolo looked at each other in horror. 'Civil war!' Alice exclaimed. 'The very worst situation any country can face.'

She looked towards Eubolo who rose and came and kissed her hand, then immediately summoned his page. So began the first steps to mobilise men-at-arms and all able-bodied troops preparatory to joining the Earl of Lancaster.

Meantime Alice sent for refreshments for Kit and plied him with further questions on the momentous events, which most certainly would alter the entire future of England.

'The queen, the Earls of Kent and Norfolk, the king's half-brothers, together with Lord Mortimer of Wigmore are in close attendance and they are to make for London with all speed.' Kit's voice was serious.

Alice nodded. 'And we can be assured that Lord Mortimer will avenge his family's harsh treatment. His wife was separated from her children and sent to Skipton Castle on a mere pittance for her upkeep and his mother was incarcerated in a nunnery.'

Kit smiled and said, 'His sons are already free, as I am sure are all of his family, along with many more who fell foul of the Despencers.'

Alice added a poignant note. 'For those lucky enough to have survived that is.'

In November, the king was captured at Neath as too were the younger Despencer and his cleric Robert Baldock. The latter pair were both found hiding in woods nearby. The Earl of Lancaster escorted the king to his own castle at Kenilworth and Eubolo sent messages that he was among the escort party. Despencer and Baldock were taken to Hereford where the queen and Mortimer, along with many magnates and prelates, made ready for their trial.

'We can be certain that he will receive a bloody end, the queen and Mortimer both have too many scores to settle for it to be otherwise. Thomas's execution will also be avenged, which must satisfy his brother.'

Matty looked up from her needlework, 'And how does that sit with you, my lady?'

Alice remained silent for some time before answering, 'Lancaster's blood is not only on the hands of the Despencers, but also on the king's. They both must share the guilt. He ignored his wife's pleas of mercy and I am certain many clerics also urged leniency. Sadly, Thomas was born to a position greater than his personal capabilities, as was the king; it is a pity that the two Plantagenet cousins should be so bitterly opposed to each other, that they brought England to civil war over their intransigent quarrels. The country now stands at a crossroads: to accept the queen or to rally to a beleaguered king.'

'Whatever the outcome, there will be blood spilt, I'll wager.'

Alice nodded. 'Sadly, Matty, that is all too true. I fear for my dearest lord's welfare in all of this!'

BOOK THREE

FORTUNE'S WHEEL

CHAPTER XXII

The Tower of London

Eleanor Despencer shivered in the wintry draughts that blew around the cold walls and under the doors of the Tower of London. The comfortable apartments she had formerly occupied had been exchanged for the forbidding chambers in which she was now confined.

She had been unceremoniously taken under armed guard to this feared prison where she knew Isabella would not look on her plight kindly, in fact quite the opposite. Now no longer under the protection of her powerful husband, whose fate she was yet to learn, Eleanor prayed that her sisters might intercede on her behalf. This fanciful hope was quite unlikely, given that she had sided with her husband in gaining much of their rightful inheritance.

Already, three of her daughters had been forcefully removed to nunneries and Eleanor knew that an even worse fate could be in store for her because of the part she had played in her husband's rise to prominence. She had lived too long in the soft lap of comfort not to feel the cold and indignities she now received from her captors. Refused writing materials, she learned of her husband's gruesome death from the tongues of gleeful guards who enjoyed baiting her with the gory details. Filled with grief, cold, hungry and alone, Eleanor spent endless hours weeping and contemplating her fate. She was haunted by the thought of the many wives and widows who had been heartlessly relieved of their lands, wealth and liberty by the orders of her husband. Was this God's punishment? Hugh and his father had both been put to death for their overbearing ambitions. Now she was being taunted by the foul-mouthed gaolers, who alleged her husband had an unnatural relationship with the king, an idea which horrified her and in which she consistently refused to believe. Ambitious, cruel maybe, but...ungodly – never!

Shamed and frightened, Eleanor was now forced to live with the gnawing doubt that possibly Hugh had been unfaithful to her – with her uncle the king. The notion was too terrible to contemplate, but it laced her waking hours and her tormented nights, filled only by frightful nightmares, when sleep refused to give her any peaceful relief. The very idea made her sick to her stomach.

Whilst Eleanor de Clare languished in the stark, cold walls of prison, the queen and Mortimer were set to bring about the end of Isabella's husband's reign. They knew that Kenilworth would prove a magnet to the few who still remained loyal to the king, but before he was moved, Adam Orleton, Bishop of Hereford and supporter of the Mortimer family, urged the king to give up his Great Seal and accept his son Edward as his successor. Although the king adamantly refused at first, he was forced to face the harsh facts of his situation and finally he submitted. Orleton, who had been among the prelates at odds with the king and Despencer over matters concerning the Church, now was only too happy to aid his patrons.

The Yuletide of 1326 was a season of merriment not only for Isabella and Mortimer but also for Alice and Eubolo who enjoyed the festivities for a variety of reasons. However, the same could not be said for the king, wretched and alone, his hours filled with grief for the loss of his dead companion and the loss of his crown.

Meantime, weeks after the festivities, her former brother-in-law Henry Plantagenet, Earl of Lancaster and Leicester, visited Alice. It was an interview Alice knew was necessary and had not been looking forward to, but she accepted that certain legal matters needed to be resolved. She wore a plain kirtle of deep green and surcoat of rich-plum velvet, edged with the de Lacy knot motif embroidered around the edges. Around the fingers of her left hand she had twisted the rosary of moonstones. She indicated to the high-backed chair which faced the busy, crackling fire.

'It has been a long time, my lord.' Her voice was low but distinct.

'Indeed, madam.' She knew Henry felt as discomforted at this meeting as did she. 'I suppose belated congratulations are in order at your marriage.'

She looked straight at him. 'Come, my lord, let not hypocrisy sit in at this meeting.'

Henry studied the slender figure of his late brother's widow; this was not the shy, quiet girl he had once known, this was a woman of maturity, self-assurance and confidence. 'My brother's death must have come as a relief.'

Alice came and sat opposite, her face serious and intent. 'You judge me thus, my lord? Your brother's death was neither sought nor wished for by me.'

'But you left him for Surrey.'

Alice suddenly smiled. 'You believe that I and Warenne were lovers?'

Henry felt deeply uncomfortable, for he was not used to being challenged, especially by a woman. 'I...only know that you left my brother's house and went to stay at Reigate, a Surrey castle.'

'And you believe I instigated such a move?'

Henry shuffled his buttocks on the leather cushion. 'It was common knowledge at the time.'

'Ah yes, but it was a move to belittle your brother's reputation, and who were those that benefited by that? Certainly not I, nor in fact Warenne; he lost Sandal together with many more lands and castles because of his part in the plan. Beside which Warenne was in love with Maud de Nereford. Even the lusty Surrey would be hard put to hold two mistresses successfully, don't you think? No, my lord, I was the pawn in the game played by the king and the Despencers and it saddens me that you choose to hold me in such low esteem.'

Henry cleared his throat. 'Maud always said she did not believe the rumours.'

'And you chose to ignore her?'

'To my shame, madam...I did.'

'Oh, it is so easy to call a woman a daughter of Eve. You above all people knew your brother's character but still chose to judge me guilty.'

'I kept well out of the perfidious actions of both the king and my brother.' He looked down and suddenly lost his commanding air as Alice glimpsed the boy she had once known. 'There is another reason why I kept my distance, which had naught to do with plots and intrigue...' He looked across at her as he spoke. 'A reason I have not even dared to acknowledge even to myself, but one which I now believe you should be privy to.' Alice indicated for Noah to bring two goblets of wine. They remained silent as the rich, red liquid was poured into the vessels. Noah moved out of earshot and Henry continued looking even more abashed.

Alice raised her goblet: 'To secrets, my lord.'

Henry drank deeply and placed the cup back onto the table. 'Quite simply I could not bear to see you married...' Here he looked down at his boots, then rushed on. 'To another.'

Alice was stunned by his admission. Then without more ado,' she walked round the table and planted a kiss on his head. 'Oh, my lord, we were but children.'

'Nevertheless, I loved you deeply,' Lancaster said, his voice husky.

'But after you married Maud your affections were...?'

'Still yours.' He caught her hand. 'Forgive me. Through my own misplaced affections I neglected to take care of you and for that I will never forgive myself.'

Alice walked to the window. 'But such feelings die with time, do they not, my lord? I always thought you and Maud made such a good match.'

He came and stood behind her and placed his hands lightly on her shoulders. 'Maud was the most dutiful wife and mother, but love cannot be commanded, lady. Believe that if you will, I have not found it so!'

She turned and looked up into his face. 'It has taken a deal of courage to tell me this now, why did you not come forward after Thomas's death?'

'I felt it would have been a betrayal of both Maud and my brother – can you understand that?'

Alice was conscious of his nearness and moved slightly. 'From you, Henry, yes I can, but now I have married a man of honour and kindness and therefore the matter is forever closed.' She smiled gently up at him. 'I always wished that you had been chosen as my husband, but Fate had another role for both of us to play and now we cannot change parts. Unlike the mummers and actors who entertain us, we are locked into our lives as surely as if we were locked into a prison cell.'

Alice did not realise how much self-control it took Henry Plantagenet not to take her in his arms, but instead he caught her hand and kissed it. 'Be happy, lady, for both of us!' And with that he turned on his heel and walked out, leaving Alice still staring out of the window. She remained motionless for some time, then turned back and picked up her unfinished wine.

That evening she merely mentioned the earl's visit in passing. The talk was full of what the queen and Mortimer's next step would be especially in connection with the king's future. Alice listened but made few comments. She tried to imagine what her father would have advised in such a situation, but events had outrun his generation and nothing would ever be quite the same again.

CHAPTER XXIII

Kenilworth Castle
1327

Eubolo LeStrange sat with his elbows resting on the trestle table, his face cupped in his hands, staring into space. His squire was busy sorting out his armour in separate piles, the silence only disturbed by the clank of metal.

'An odd state of affairs, Tom!' Eubolo exclaimed. 'Two kings, yet one now not a king.'

'Aye, my lord!' Tom Chetwode replied, continuing with sorting the damaged armour into a pile ready to be collected for repair. 'It is indeed a unique situation and I have heard the Earl of Lancaster does not like the king's father being held here at Kenilworth.' Eubolo turned and looked at his squire, noting the sturdy frame, shock of dark hair and neat, strong hands. He had chosen Tom as his squire only six months prior to their being summoned into Earl Henry of Lancaster's household. Formerly Eubolo had served his brother Thomas but his family had not supported the ill-fated earl in his opposition to the king mainly because they also hated the Despencers.

Tom Chetwode was the bastard son of Sir John Chetwode of Chetwynd, an estate lying only a few miles from Cheswardine Castle held by the LeStrange family. Oddly enough the two had never previously met, but they quickly formed a bond after Tom entered Eubolo's service; for him, Eubolo was a noted warrior, and his skill with the sword made him the boy's hero. On Eubolo's side he had come to appreciate Tom's willingness to listen and learn, but chiefly his quiet manner and discretion. He knew the lad practised diligently long after the other squires had retired to their beds. It was a trait Eubolo understood and recognised as one he had had when he was a squire. Tom's eye for detail and methodical routine had brought an order and reliability to Eubolo's military harness essential in times of war. The boy had wit and intelligence and Eubolo was certain he would rise in the ranks more quickly than many more privileged sons of the nobility.

Eubolo was preparing to watch the latest group of squires. But there was an underlying urgency in the day's training, for rumours had begun to circulate that the former king's adherents were about to try and free him from his imprisonment here at Kenilworth.

It was the reason Henry of Lancaster paced up and down his chamber. He did not like his role as gaoler, but as Steward of England, he had been the obvious choice. However, it was one he would gladly relinquish with relief. Henry pondered over the recent appointment of mentors to the young King Edward III, which had conspicuously omitted Roger Mortimer of Wigmore, for undoubtedly it was his authority which was in overall control, as his close relationship to the queen ensured. Would this alliance result in a similar situation to the one so recently overthrown? The role once held by Despencer would now be filled by a damned Welsh Marcher baron. Henry ground his teeth in his agitation. The Mortimers were feared and hated by the Welsh and the earl did not wish to find himself once more on a field of battle facing yet another civil uprising.

The earl paced up and down, his mind troubled by the fate of Edward II. It was a dangerous situation having an anointed king still alive, even though he *had* reluctantly surrendered his seals of office to his eldest son, but for the present Henry of Lancaster had to fulfil his role as gaoler to his former king, whatever his personal feelings on the circumstances.

Some months later the king's father was taken secretly to Berkeley Castle. This was thought necessary as rumours of a plot to free him had begun to circulate. Henry cared little for the reasoning; he only felt a sense of relief at being rid of his royal prisoner – although there were still many outstanding matters which concerned him, not least his position with Roger Mortimer, Baron of Wigmore, for their quarrel was becoming ever more vociferous.

Fortune, however, smiled more kindly on Alice and Eubolo as their lives became far more settled. Alice reclaimed castles and lands once held by her mother's family, which had not been part of her marriage contract with the late Thomas of Lancaster. Eubolo was being recognised for his own merits and now took his place when parliament was called. However, he had adamantly refused to accept the title of Earl of Lincoln and Salisbury which he was entirely entitled to do. It had amused Alice when she had made the suggestion that he should become Earl of Lincoln and she had seen the expression change on her husband's face.

'Oh, my dearest Eubolo, please do not think that you are obliged to take the title if it does not suit you.'

He had sighed with relief. 'The title of countess is yours by right of birth but mine... I will not use a title I have not earned although I am more than honoured. It is just...'

'Think no more of it. I wish you to feel comfortable and we will say no more on the matter.'

During the next few years the struggle for power which Henry of Lancaster had foreseen did indeed erupt, and it became ever more evident that it was Mortimer who pulled the strings of government, endorsed by the willing Isabella. Rumours of their personal relationship had also begun to circulate and there was speculation that they were lovers.

The growing divisions of loyalty finally came to a head when a plot to free Edward II implicated the hapless Edmund, Earl of Kent, one of his sons by Margaret of France. The ruthless action taken to have him executed for treason aroused outrage in the country and Mortimer was judged guilty by many of the magnates for carrying out such a harsh sentence on a royal earl. Once more England teetered on the edge of civil war.

The situation was exacerbated by what some named the 'Shameful Treaty' with Scotland, whereby Robert the Bruce was finally recognised as the King of Scotland and a lasting peace negotiated on Mortimer's advice. That years of conflict had been brought to an ignominious finale stemmed mainly from the fact that England had precious little money in the coffers.

Soon after, Mortimer was created Earl of March. This just added fuel to the fires of resentment and the erstwhile Baron of Wigmore did nothing to endear himself to his peers. He and Isabella began to award themselves vast sums of silver and landholdings, added to which Mortimer had married many of his sons and daughters to the wealthiest and most prestigious families in the land.

The young king became ever more furious at Mortimer's attitude. He frequently walked in front of both Isabella and Edward, displaying no sign of deference towards either of them. This outward show of arrogance infuriated Edward so much he secretly began forming a party of young nobles to oppose Mortimer's rule. Patiently he bided his time and wrote secretly to Rome. The son of an inept and shameful king had inherited the characteristics of his grandsire, not his sire, and he was not about to see the throne usurped by anyone, least of all Mortimer.

Isabella failed to note her son's festering resentment at Mortimer's influence over her. She blindly trusted the man whom she had come to rely on for both her emotional decisions and the decisions of the realm. The couple were so lost in their relationship that when the young king made his move to regain control of his kingdom, they realised they had been fatally outmanoeuvred.

In the autumn of 1330 at Nottingham Castle, Edward and his friends secretly entered the apartments occupied by Mortimer and his mother and after a bloody fight the earl was taken prisoner and hauled once more to the Tower of London, his fate already sealed. Once again, the Mortimer family found themselves imprisoned, paying the price for the head of their family's actions.

Mortimer's shameful death at Tyburn was felt most bitterly by his wife, Joan de Geneville, who had been cuckolded by her husband with the queen and was now being punished yet again, but Joan never ceased to love her husband. She had seen the change in him on his return to England and judged him not as others did.

They had been parted for almost five years since he had been taken prisoner and incarcerated in the Tower of London. She knew how he must have fretted over his family's imprisonment, which must have eaten at his very being. Any animal cornered and wounded, especially one defending its young, could prove a vicious force of nature and would use its fangs; in the same way Roger had suffered both taunts and injuries and had used his 'fangs' on anyone judged his enemy. Regretfully, he had become drunk with his heady position of power, paying the ultimate penalty with his execution.

His body was left shamefully hanging naked on a rope in punishment, a warning to the world that Edward III, like his grandsire, was not a monarch who was afraid to take decisive action when he saw fit.

However others judged her erring husband, Joan prayed for his soul and awaited an opportunity to reclaim his body. He was her husband and father of her children, whilst Isabella had been a mere passion of the flesh.

As for the hapless queen – she was taken to Berkhampstead Castle, distraught at Mortimer's capture. On hearing of his execution, she broke down inconsolably, her world crashing down as her son now took full control of his own destiny, replacing those in power with his trusted adherents.

He had commissioned Eubolo to be in charge of his mother's removal to Berkhampstead. LeStrange was somewhat nonplussed on how to deal with this delicate situation. He sent for Alice to help and in the midst of winter she found herself riding through inclement weather in response to her husband's plea.

After a horse lost a shoe delaying their journey, it was almost dark when the party rode through the castle gates. Eubolo had sent guards out to locate them, being worried at the lateness of the hour. Together the group arrived, tired, cold but safe.

Alice declined refreshments, preferring to seek information on how she could be of assistance to her husband.

'In all honesty, I am so relieved to see you, my dearest.' He held her cold hands as he spoke. 'Isabella is refusing to allow anyone in to her apartment. She refuses food, even warmth; her wails can at times be heard around the castle. I truly fear for her sanity.'

Alice shook her head. 'This cannot continue! Leave it to me. I will endeavour to speak with her and see if I can make her see reason.'

Eubolo kissed her hand. 'I felt certain you would know how to deal with the poor woman.'

Removing her heavy travelling cloak, Alice asked to be taken to the queen's apartments directly. Outside the door, she found a group of servants who were obviously uncertain what to do. The sound of sobbing could be heard plainly coming from within.

They bowed at Alice's approach.

She turned. 'Who are the queen's personal servants?' A young woman and a squire stepped forward. Alice indicated to a page to join them.

'I want to know the last time the queen ate.'

The woman curtseyed before she spoke, 'I am Amy Gaveston.

My duty is as lady of the bedchamber. Alas, her personal maid refuses to enter the queen's chamber… I am the only one! The queen hasn't eaten for nigh on five days. I have tried everything, but she dashes the food to floor and now will allow no one into her presence.'

Alice spoke softly, 'What I will try to do is gain entry. Once I have succeeded, then I will need you to listen my orders.' She turned to the page. 'You will be in charge of lighting the fire. Bring enough kindling for the night.' She looked at the young woman. 'When I call for refreshments I want you to have warmed milk laced with honey ready to be served with a tray of tasty morsels.' She smiled at the rest of the group. 'You can all go to bed now!'

Without further ado, Alice walked to the heavy oak-studded door, turned the handle and walked in. A look of apprehension passed between the waiting servants.

Alice stood for a moment, her eyes scanning the darkness, for only a single rushlight flickered in a sconce on the far wall. On the bed lay the crumpled figure of Isabella of France. Suddenly aware she was no longer alone she raised her head, her voice thick with grief. 'Out, do you dare to disobey your queen?'

'Is this how you greet your guests?' Isabella peered at the shadowy figure.

'Guests are invited. I have invited no one.'

Alice walked further into the chamber. 'Do your servants leave you to freeze?'

'My servants obey me, pray kindly do the same.'

Alice walked over to the bed. 'Do you really expect me to leave you in such reduced circumstances?'

A look of recognition dawned on Isabella's face. 'Countess of Lincoln, has my son sent you to spy on me?'

Alice pulled a chair closer to the bed and sat down before replying. 'Is that what you believe, that I am a spy for your son?' She smiled wanly. 'I have come at the behest of my husband who is in charge of your wellbeing.' Alice's eyes were slowly becoming accustomed to the gloom. Isabella looked hollow-eyed, her hair tangled, her clothes dishevelled. 'You need a fire and more light.' She paused, waiting for Isabella's reaction, then continued, 'I find as I get older it is more difficult to keep warm.' There was no reply. Alice knew if she did not take charge now Isabella would either die of cold and hunger, or go insane and be confined forever, for which Eubolo would be blamed. She racked her brains to find a way of reaching the bereaved woman.

'Do you believe you are the only woman to be left grieving? After Bannockburn, there were thousands of families mourning the loss of loved ones.' Alice was aware that Isabella had risen to a sitting position.

'Do you think it is merely grief I feel? Shame, bitter, cruel shame gnaws at my body and soul, it fills my mouth, destroys my mind.' The words were punctuated by sobs.

Alice moved towards the weeping figure and gathered her in her arms. She felt Isabella tense for moment, then she hid her face in Alice's neck and wept. Alice stroked the thick mass of tangled hair, murmuring softly. 'Do you believe the shame to be yours alone?'

The answer was a strangled 'Yes! Yes! Yes!'

'Well, I do not!'

Isabella raised her head to look into Alice's face, her expression one of disbelief. 'Explain, I prithee.'

'An explanation would be made easier if I had a fire to heat my hands and a drink to warm my stomach. I have travelled many miles this day.'

Isabella nodded. Gently Alice disentangled herself from Isabella's arms and moved to the door. She called to the page and signalled towards the figure of Amy Gaveston. The boy quickly entered the room and within moments had a blaze busily burning in the fireplace. He left without a word. A little while later there was a gentle knock. Amy entered the room carrying a tray laden with two cups of steaming milk accompanied by dainty morsels of game pie, cold chicken, fruit and sweetmeats. She curtseyed leaving the two women alone once more. Alice noted how like Piers Amy was in looks, though she seemed to possess none of her father's haughtiness.

Alice handed Isabella the cup of milk before returning to her seat. Isabella sipped the warming liquid. 'Now will you explain?'

'It is difficult trying to put into a few words the long list of mistakes, misunderstandings, fears and jealousies. It is hard to know exactly where to begin. Maybe it is easier to work backwards. I will start with the period when your husband fell under the influence of Despencer. As king it was his duty to seek good counsel on matters of state. His bad judgement allowed Despencer and his family almost total control and their dictates brought the country to a sorry state.'

Alice paused to see if Isabella was listening but she was satisfied that she had gained her whole attention. She continued slowly, 'Alienating you from your husband, the king from his subjects, with acts which shamed the nation, simply showed his judgement to be flawed. Together, they heaped shame upon the throne of England. I always judged the so-called 'miracles' at Thomas's tomb a shrewd move by the bishop. Sadly, your son has inherited a throne of shame, but the shame is not of your making.'

Isabella stared into the cup, which she twisted round in her hand. She was beginning to realise how cold she was. 'Pray continue,' she said softly.

Alice cleared her throat before saying more. 'I am convinced it all started with the quarrels betwixt Lancaster and your husband. We who have both been married to Plantagenets know how unpredictable their nature can be. Their selfish pride resulted in England's civil war. Was that of your making? Was it of my making? I think not!' She hesitated, as speaking about long-buried issues was now proving difficult for her. 'There is one thing I wish to thank you for: pleading for Lancaster's life.' Isabella lifted her tear-stained face. A look of amazement etched her once beautiful face.

'You must have hated him?' Isabella's question hung in the air.

Alice rose and walked up and down before returning to the fireside. In a low voice she almost whispered, 'But I never wished Lancaster dead. Someone far wiser than I taught me that hatred is a double-edged weapon, one which can destroy the one who hates.'

'But you left?'

Alice smiled sadly, 'Oh yes, I left, for my own safety and self-respect.'

Isabella's curiosity was obvious. 'Even though you knew you would be condemned by the Church and society.' Her voice was thick and husky from the many hours of weeping.

'Sometimes you must follow the dictates of your own conscience. Is that not what we are taught, be true to yourself and you will then be true to God?' Alice gazed into the fire as she spoke.

Isabella rubbed her aching eyes. 'Do you really believe that I will not be looked on with contempt?' She stared hard at Alice as she spoke.

'If you feel you are contemptible then, yes, that is how you will be treated. In my opinion, you were the only legitimate opponent to challenge Despencer, which took a great deal of courage.' Alice hesitated, searching for the right words. 'Was I correct? Did you do it for the sake of your son as well as for yourself?'

Isabella's eyes filled with tears. 'I watched my husband fall deeper and deeper into the clutches of that despicable Despencer family. I truly believed Hugh would have me killed when the right opportunity arose. He feared France – he feared my ties with the Church and my popularity with the people.'

Isabella rose slowly and came to join Alice before the fire, which was now glowing warmly in the hearth. 'When Mortimer came and offered his services…' She began to sob, regaining her control after a moment or two. 'I little realised we would also fall in love.' Again a muffled sob. 'Now he is dead and I am left to…' She began weeping again.

Alice came and knelt before the grieving woman. 'Now you must pick up your courage once more. You are the daughter of a king – were married to a king and are mother to a king. Your son is still too young to realise all the pitfalls ruling a nation entails. You must place the needs of your son before all others – even your own.' Alice paused, knowing what she was about to say could influence Isabella's future. 'Even if he does not openly seek your advice he will need your support. There will be times when he is offered two paths of action both seemingly feasible, but with vastly differing outcomes. This will be when he will need your experience, not openly or even knowingly, but the need will be there and, as a queen, surely it is your duty to be there for him? After all, is that not the role of a mother?'

A burning log fell in the fire causing a finger of smoke to rise and curl up the chimney. For then what seemed a very long time silence cloaked the chamber. Isabella finally rose, paced slowly for a time, then stopped to face Alice. 'Are you the only one who does not attach any blame or shame to me?'

'No, your name has never been linked to any shame.'

Isabella groaned. 'So all the blame is…was my poor Mortimer's?'

'Who has paid the debt with his life. Do not let his death go in vain,' Alice said quietly. Again the chamber fell into silence.

'No doubt you will report this conversation to my son?'

'Why do you say that? All we have spoken of tonight remains within the walls of this chamber. I will not even speak of it with my husband.' Alice reached out and grasped Isabella's icy hands. 'I judge you not, that is for God alone. Besides, do we not judge ourselves far more severely than others?' Then, with a wry smile playing around her lips, she resumed, 'However, I fear your confessor may have plans for a prolonged penance for you.'

Isabella looked at Alice. 'I do not know how I will feel on the morrow. However, I will consider all we have talked about this night. When I feel a need to speak about Mortimer and the past, can I send for you?'

Alice rose, then dropped a curtsey.

'You are the Dowager Queen Mother and as such can command my presence.'

'Alice de Lacy, I will never utter such a command, but if I send for you as a friend?'

'Then as a friend I will be only too pleased to accept. Now may I tell your attendants that you will no longer send them away?'

Isabella nodded, then came and kissed Alice's cheek. 'Thank you, countess, I little realised how I was in need of comfort. Your words will remain with me forever.' Alice returned the kiss, dropped a curtsey then turned and left the royal apartments.

As she walked through the long passageways she felt suddenly very tired, but satisfied that in some small way she might have brought comfort to the distraught queen. Upon entering the apartment Eubolo rose and as he was about to speak, Alice raised her hand. 'Suffice it to say Isabella has allowed her servants to attend her. Now I am weary, cold and famished.'

Eubolo kissed his wife's brow. 'I knew if anyone could resolve the situation, my dearest Alice could.'

Edward III was a true Plantagenet in looks and stature and to all of those close to him he displayed the attributes needed to succeed as a powerful king. Through his formative years he had witnessed the power-play by his father's favourites, had seen the quarrel between his uncle Thomas of Lancaster grow out of all proportion, stoked by the ambitions of the Despencers, had watched the shameful behaviour of his mother – all those things had imprinted themselves upon his consciousness. Now he was about to show the world that a new era had begun, with an English king that was both just and powerful and who would act according to the best interests of his kingdom and not at the behest of favourites. Edward was married to Phillipa of Hainault, who had presented him with a son and heir, which they also named Edward. The House of Plantagenet was about to emerge once more from the shameful years, the throne of shame replaced by a throne of honour.

Eubolo and Alice found themselves amongst those serving the king frequently on delicate matters of state. Sometimes it involved them either escorting the dowager queen to court or simply acting as messengers on more secret missions.

Throughout the next five years the couple's place in society was one of respect and influence. It was a period when Alice felt most secure and Eubolo's devotion never wavered. The couple acted as one in so many matters.

Finally Matty felt her prayers for Alice had been fulfilled. Nowadays, as age began to take its toll, she was helped by a girl from the Stapelton household named Annie who did the more strenuous duties, leaving Matty to her needlework even though her eyesight was beginning to fail.

The couple moved to Bolingbroke as their main home but frequently visited Ellesmere, Canford and Lincoln. Alice's visits to court were infrequent even though she had established a friendly relationship with the young Queen Phillipa, but she also visited the dowager queen. Alice worked tirelessly to improve conditions for the poor and her reputation as a benefactress quickly grew. However, the income due from Lincoln was consistently refused, resulting in a court case whereby an order from the king eventually resolved the stalemate in their favour.

Edward III's reputation was growing as a just and able ruler both in England and on the Continent. His queen became a favourite of the people. Phillipa was no great beauty, unlike her mother-in-law, but her kindness proved a valuable asset where popularity was concerned. Isabella, although she no longer held any real powers, was frequently present on state occasions. Her relationship with her grandchildren also blossomed, especially with the young Prince Edward.

In 1335 Eubolo was called on to serve once more in Scotland. Robert the Bruce had been dead almost six years, but hostilities had once more flared up, requiring the king to take decisive action to quell the uprising. As Alice bade Eubolo farewell she felt fear clutch at her heart. She hated being parted from her beloved husband, but his reassurances helped allay her fears. As the troops assembled Alice indicated to Tom to watch over his master. In response he kissed his thumb and made the sign of the cross on his breast, signalling that he understood her request.

Late in September, a mud-besplattered messenger galloped a weary horse through the gates of Bolingbroke Castle with devastating news from Scotland. Eubolo was dead and Tom seriously wounded, how seriously was not yet known. There had been a fierce battle near Stirling and the sketchy facts implied that it was near the castle that the Lord Eubolo had fallen. Alice felt as though she too had been wounded, the pain of grief unbearable in its intensity. She felt bereft, shattered, broken, the light of life dimmed forever.

Some weeks later, Eubolo's body returned to Bolingbroke, escorted by his wounded squire. Tom and Alice wept bitter tears, as did the entire LeStrange household. Matty feared for her mistress as grief plunged Alice into a deep pit which excluded the rest of the world. She scarcely ate and often wandered the castle during the hours of the night, unable to find any rest. Daytime found her dark-eyed on her knees in her chapel, praying fervently.

When Tom's severe wounds began to heal he recounted the actual sequence of the battle. Eubolo's horse had been brought down and as he struggled to free himself he received a sword thrust which rendered him helpless. As Tom had fought his way to his master's side, he too had been wounded and had lost consciousness. When he came to, Eubolo was dead and his body was being carried to a Scottish stronghold. Tom had only received some rough nursing and his wound had become infected, hence his almost delirious condition when he arrived home. Alice held his hand and whispered, 'Your life was saved by Simon who purged the poisons from your system.'

When the necessary arrangements had been made, Eubolo's funeral was held at Barlings Abbey and he was laid to rest within its grounds. It was one of the saddest days in Alice's life trying to remain composed whilst bidding her dearest husband goodbye.

But Annie gave thanks to God for sparing Tom's life, for she had been in love with him for some while.

In the following months Alice was given precious little time to mourn. If she believed her trials were behind her, the events which followed proved otherwise. However, she was quite correct about the ambitions of men, and a name from the past was about to cause Alice even greater heartache. Hugh de Freyne, who deserted Lancaster some months before Boroughbridge, had over the intervening years made his living by selling his services to the highest fee-payer. He had recently fought in Scotland where he learned of LeStrange's death.

Upon his return he discovered Alice's situation and saw his chance to further his fortunes. It was not uncommon for wealthy widows to be abducted. In fact, Elizabeth de Clare had recently found herself in similar circumstances. Once compromised, the reputation of the unfortunate woman was only restored after they were forcibly married to their abductors, a situation which seemed to be condoned by the Church.

Just as Alice had decided to take a vow of chastity and retire to the abbey at Barlings to be closer to her late husband, she found herself at the mercy of Hugh de Freyne. During the initial attack she fought like a wild cat as did Matty, but de Freyne and his thugs were too strong and when she was threatened that if she did not cease her struggle, they would kill Noah and Tom, both brutally injured whilst trying to defend their mistress, she submitted without further struggle.

Both Alice and Matty were unceremoniously bundled onto the back of a horse, causing Matty to give vent to her fury, so much so that a kerchief was stuffed into her mouth to silence her curses. Alice threw herself to the ground from her horse, but de Freyne had her tied to one of his servants who rode pillion, holding her on as they sped swiftly through the night.

Bruised and bleeding, Alice once again found herself the victim of a brutal rape. Scalding tears coursed down her battered face, and she prayed that death would release her from her prison, but neither God nor the king listened to her pleas for mercy. She was horrified when the king sanctioned the marriage to de Freyne, leaving Alice once more at the mercy of a ruthless man.

Matty watched the spirit die in Alice and once more vowed

to help her mistress with whatever means she could, relying on neither God nor man. Matty decided to turn once more to the ancient arts, which she had used for her mistress in the past. What did it matter if she lost her immortal soul, it was a price worth paying to help her beloved mistress. Matty bided her time; she wanted no repercussions falling on her mistress or for that matter herself. She laid her plans without even discussing them with Alice, for she knew she would try to dissuade her. Besides, Alice had withdrawn into a world where no one could reach her.

As the summer faded into autumn, Matty collected the root of the mandrake plant mixed in a basket of mushrooms, which she hid until she could use them for her deadly purpose. She experimented in many ways on how to hide the bitter taste by disguising it in a variety of tasty mushroom dishes. Finally at the end of October she rubbed her hands in satisfaction as she produced a nourishing, warming dish with some of the ancient spices from the east. She smiled. 'This special relish will make the dish an unforgettable feast,' she murmured to herself. The trick now was not to poison the whole household and for that she engaged the talents of Hywel, the unsuspecting Welsh musician.

On the chosen date, the smells rising from the kitchens were tongue-watering and everyone was looking forward to the evening's feast. Matty sat quietly waiting for her chance and when Hywel began a toe-tapping tune, urging the company to clap in time to the music, Matty slid the phial from her large sleeve into the dish that was just about to be handed to Lord de Freyne. Matty had cleverly added other herbs and potions to slow the action of the poison, and it was not until the following day when Alice was out riding that a messenger galloped up to inform her that her husband was dead.

Her eyes opened wide at the news. 'How so?'

'He just fell over clutching his heart, his eyes rolling. His tongue had turned blue.'

The physician pronounced failure of his heart. Matty smiled, thankful that the physician had been Simon who would never betray either her or her mistress.

Upon Alice's return she called Matty to her solar. 'God has finally listened,' Alice said softly, 'although the messenger was somewhat tardy in carrying your message.'

Matty said, her head turned so that Alice could not read her expression, 'Always trust in God, my lady, he is our shield and our sword.'

'A somewhat odd expression, Matty!' Alice exclaimed.

'Nevertheless, did he not strike the Parasites?'

Alice smiled. 'I think you mean the Pharisees.' She stopped. 'Well, maybe he did remove the parasite. He does move in mysterious ways.' It was the first time for months that Alice appeared to be herself.

After de Freyne's funeral, Alice and Matty journeyed back to Bolingbroke. Within days they came under attack, their attackers being none other than Roger LeStrange and her bastard brother John de Lacy. The attack was so vicious it left two of her servants dead and her best horses stolen. Josh, the young groom, had been wounded trying to save them. To Alice this was the final blow; her rage erupted like a volcano, with an intensity never before witnessed by Matty.

'I tell you, Matty, I will be avenged of this heinous crime. How dare that cur de Lacy raise his hand against me, his own blood? What code of honour does he follow? And as for the LeStrange cove – I curse him to hell. Is this how my husband's family treat a grieving widow? If it hadn't been for the quick actions of Noah in fetching the sheriff I hesitate to think what the outcome of the day would have been.' She paced angrily up and down, fire burning in her pale eyes and her fists clenched and beating into each other. 'I tell you, Matty, I renounce the world, for money, land and titles are all these men ever want. It burns my very heart to think that the best of men lies in the cold earth when the likes of these...' She waved her arms helplessly in the air like broken flails off a windmill. Matty waited for the tears to follow, but Alice remained angry and restless.

The sheriff had ordered the LeStrange party away from the castle with a warning that should they return they would face serious consequences and the matter would be brought to court where an impartial jury would decide on the rights and wrongs of the matter.

So Alice found herself alone once more facing the ambitions and avarice of men whose hostile demeanour she found neither frightening nor intimidating, for she was at war. The deep hurt she felt inside at her loss was such that whatever words and threats were set against her she merely shrugged off. This infuriated her adversaries. But the court found in her favour and she left with her head held high. As she passed LeStrange and her bastard brother, she stopped and the look of sheer contempt which crossed her features was a sight Matty would never forget.

Sadly the horses, which had been returned by order of the court, were physical wrecks, and she wept at their wretched state. Her favourite riding horse was so lame she feared it would have to be destroyed, but Josh, who was still bandaged from his own wounds, urged her to allow him to try his healing skills. Simon's advice was also sought and together the health of the horses slowly began to recover.

Eventually, Alice and Matty made the journey to Barlings Abbey where Alice took a vow of chastity, determined to live out the rest of her life in a manner she herself had chosen.

The years passed swiftly, but she followed the fortunes of the king with as much interest as ever. The Mortimers were restored to their lands and titles and although Roger's son died young, he died in the service of his king. Edward restored the reputation of the Plantagenets by transforming the former throne of shame into a throne of honour and glory. His son, known as the 'Black Prince', later gained a great victory at a place called Crécy, in France.

However, it was not all good news as a pernicious disease dubbed the 'Black Death' was brought back across the Channel in ships containing many of the king's troops. It decimated the population of almost every town, village and hamlet in the land. 'Fortune's wheel spins, and men, women and children are affected in its path.' Alice spoke almost to herself. Matty knew that Alice was also failing and nearing the end of her life; daily she was becoming visibly more frail but never complained.

As they sat together one afternoon, Alice held Matty's hand. 'Thank you for all your years of devotion. My life would have been so empty without your love. Pray tell me why you never returned to Pendle, I know you longed to see your homeland again.'

Matty hesitated for a moment. 'Many years ago I came into the service of a little girl who had lost her brothers and whose heart was broken. She was lonely as was I. That day I gave you my heart and my love. Nothing has changed; you still have all my love.

Events may not have served us too well at times, but I believe we have found comfort in each other and overcome the ambitions of men.'

Alice nodded. She looked across at Matty. 'The final wound was de Freyne. I had given up all hope and would have happily died.'

Matty patted her hand. 'I know, my lady – I know!'

'Will you return to Pendle when I am no more?'

Matty nodded, hiding the tears which filled her eyes.

Alice's grip suddenly tightened. 'I shall be with Eubolo once again, he was ever a true and loving man. I was lucky to have known him even though I had to wait a long time for his arrival.' The two women smiled at each other.

A few weeks later Alice slipped quietly from life to rejoin the only man she had ever loved. Matty placed the moonstone rosary in her hands as the coffin lid closed. At her simple funeral, Matty, now old and infirm, sat quietly mourning her beloved mistress. She looked around the vaulted building to see Tom and Annie who were married with a young family. Kit Cavendish, still looking handsome, although now grey, stood beside his wife Blanche, the comely merchant's daughter. Noah had inherited his father's farm and only recently been widowed. The nuns now employed Josh in their stables, where he tended the horses. Luke Lytton, his once tall frame stooped and holding a staff, smiled across at her. He had retired from Alice's service when his eyesight began to fail. Matty nodded; she was well pleased that they had all managed to make the journey for their final farewells.

As Alice was laid to rest beside her husband, Matty made the sign of the cross. 'Forgive me my sins, O Lord, but I did keep my promise to watch over this most beloved of women who often suffered grievously at the hands of men. I submit myself to your punishment – that is if you think me guilty.' She smiled mischievously up at the heavens as she spoke.

Two weeks later Matty headed back to her homeland of Pendle to live with her sister's daughter and husband. She finally found her peace on earth and passed away whilst nursing one of the brood of children whom she had come to love, though the place in her heart which had been Alice de Lacy's was never filled by anyone else.

AUTHOR'S NOTE

The life of Alice de Lacy highlights the situation many noble women had to suffer throughout the medieval period, when they were often used as pawns by families to increase their wealth and status. The fact that Alice lost both of her brothers in childhood meant she became sole heiress to a considerable fortune which Edward I was eager to bring into his family. The marriage arranged for Alice and the king's nephew was looked on as a mutually beneficial arrangement for both parties.

Throne of Shame is a portrayal of Alice as I see her. Many historians and chroniclers mention Alice, some in a detrimental light, but in the comprehensive work by Professor Seymour Phillips, *Edward II*, he holds the opinion that Alice was used as a royal pawn and her first 'abduction' by John de Warenne was a means of undermining Lancaster and was not carried out because she and Warenne were lovers.

Most accounts state that the marriage of Alice and Lancaster was a disastrous one and that they divorced in 1316/7. If this were in fact the case, I find it somewhat puzzling that neither remarried during the following years of Lancaster's life, and the question must be asked: if Alice and Eubolo were lovers prior to this time, why did they not marry upon Alice obtaining a divorce? It was actually two and a half years after Lancaster's execution before they married. *Alice's reputation certainly suffered during this period being linked to two lovers, Eubolo and Warenne!*

There is also another reason to question the divorce: why was Alice accused of Lancaster's treason immediately after his execution if there had been a lawful divorce? She appears to have had no contact with him during the years 1316 to 1322, so why was she held responsible for his crimes? Of course, this may have been Despencer's way of parting Alice from much of her remaining lands and fortune by his favoured method of intimidation.

The fate of Alice after Eubolo's death was shocking: being abducted and raped whilst she was deep in mourning must have been traumatic and sickening. It counts as a truly shameful act on the part of Hugh de Freyne, who appeared to care nothing for Alice as a person, only for her status. His sudden death has been laid at Alice's door in some historical sources, which also blamed her for the deaths of her brothers. I have totally discounted these accusations. Other references on her character say Alice was a benefactress. Also, she was involved in few lawsuits brought by tenants – this points to a woman capable of administering her estates without redress to the law, a remarkable achievement when you look at all the lawsuits there were involving lands and tenancies during that period.

I can only hazard a guess at Alice's reactions when reports of miracles at Lancaster's tomb began to circulate. He was by all accounts a religious man – which sits at odds with his character, but then he did donate large sums of silver to the Church, maybe to buy his heavenly salvation. To my mind, the Church used these 'miracles' to embarrass the king and Despencer after a dispute between Church and State.

Another interesting fact connected with Lancaster's execution is the murder of Robert Holland close to an estate once owned by Lancaster. No one was brought to trial over his death, which leaves me wondering whether Lancaster's brother Henry took his revenge on Holland for deserting his brother. The truth may lie in the long-held resentment of local gentry who lost lands to Holland during the time he was in service to the earl.

Throne of Shame is my tribute to a woman who withstood all the cruel ambitions of powerful men in one of English history's most turbulent eras and who, through all her adversities, retained her own self-integrity. Alice outlived virtually all of those who had brought fear and pain into her life and died at Barling Priory close to her beloved Eubolo.

Lightning Source UK Ltd.
Milton Keynes UK
UKOW050056191012

200826UK00001B/5/P